# NOTHING LIKE THE SUN

## PETER ELLISON

Hodder & Stoughton

LONDON  SYDNEY  AUCKLAND  TORONTO

**Photographic acknowledgements**

The publishers would like to thank the following for their kind permission to reproduce photographs in this volume:

Sally and Richard Greenhill (pp. 1, 41, 159); John Walmsley (pp. 9, 27); © Rapho Agence de Presse Photographique for 'Environ de Paris', 1932 by Édouard Boubat (p. 52); © Magnum Photos Ltd for 'Arrival of Jewish immigrants from Europe, Haifa harbour, Israel, May–June 1949' by Robert Capa (pp. 58–9); Popperfoto for the photograph of Port-au-Prince, Haiti (p. 68); Topham Picture Library (p. 77); © Christian Bonnington (p. 93); The Royal Photographic Society, Bath/The Trustees of the Ansel Adams Publishing Rights Trust for 'Aspens New Mexico' by Ansel Adams. All rights reserved (p. 99); J. Allan Cash Ltd (pp. 105, 110); © Magnum Photos Ltd/Guy Le Querrec (pp. 116–17); © Magnum Photos Ltd/Donald McCullin (p. 121); Bradford Enterprise Service (pp. 128–9); © Syndication International Ltd/Paul Hamann (p. 137); © Magnum Photos Ltd/Elliott Erwitt (p. 159); © Richard Smith 1990/Katz Pictures from *The Independent*, 7 April 1990 (pp. 164–5); © Joan Klatchko/Hutchison Library (p. 168); © Bernard Gérard/Hutchison Library (p. 169); Bill Travers/Zoo Check (pp. 174–5); Hanson Caroll/Robert Harding Picture Library (p. 180); Chris Gilbert (p. 184).

British Library Cataloguing in Publication Data
Nothing like the sun : an anthology of non-fiction for GCSE and standard
    grade.
    1. Great Britain. Secondary schools. Curriculum subjects:
    English language. Comprehension
    I. Ellison, Peter
    428.20712

ISBN 0 340 51894 4

First published 1990

Typeset by Wearside Tradespools, Fulwell, Sunderland

Printed for the educational publishing division of Hodder and Stoughton, Mill Road, Dunton Green, Sevenoaks, Kent by St Edmundsbury Press Ltd, Bury St Edmunds, Suffolk.

# Contents

# *Preface*

The title comes from Shakespeare's sonnet CXXX in praise of truthfulness:

> My mistress' eyes are nothing like the sun;
> Coral is far more red than her lips' red;
> If snow be white, why then her breasts are dun;
> If hairs be wires, black wires grow on her head:
> I have seen roses damask'd, red and white,
> But no such roses see I in her cheeks;
> And in some perfumes is there more delight
> Than in the breath that from my mistress reeks:
> I love to hear her speak, yet well I know
> That music hath a far more pleasing sound;
> I grant I never saw a goddess go, —
> My mistress when she walks treads on the ground.
>     And yet by heaven I think my love as rare
>     As any she belied with false compare.

# How to use this book

The various aspects of non-fiction are split into units:

**Units One and Two** – Autobiography, including early memories of childhood, school and first love.

**Unit Three** – Travel and reportage, including accounts of life in prison and experiences on an expedition to Borneo.

**Unit Four** – Descriptive writing.

**Unit Five** – Journalistic investigation, including the last days of a prisoner sentenced to death and the diary of a woman who takes a job as a bunnygirl.

**Unit Six** – Persuasive and discursive writing, including a discussion of the pros and cons of zoos and an article on the effects of watching TV.

Each unit contains:

- a choice of ideas for group discussion
- suggestions for class follow-up.
- a variety of suggestions for written assignments suitable for GCSE and Standard Grade coursework
- an extension section which provides ideas for wider study

## To the student

Every piece of writing that you intend to enter as coursework should be extensively drafted and re-drafted. Before a book like this is published, it has been through a number of drafts. These are written by the author but he or she takes advice from an editor because it is often difficult for us to spot our own mistakes and to see which passages could be written more clearly. Your editor is often your teacher, but this does not have to be the case. You may like to work with a partner or group who will act as your editors. You, of course, will edit for them in turn.

**Your drafting should follow this pattern:**

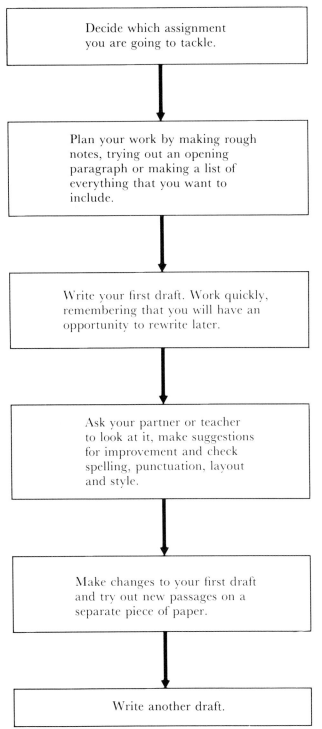

Decide which assignment you are going to tackle.

Plan your work by making rough notes, trying out an opening paragraph or making a list of everything that you want to include.

Write your first draft. Work quickly, remembering that you will have an opportunity to rewrite later.

Ask your partner or teacher to look at it, make suggestions for improvement and check spelling, punctuation, layout and style.

Make changes to your first draft and try out new passages on a separate piece of paper.

Write another draft.

# 1

# MEMORIES AND MOMENTS

# Autobiographical writing

One of the special appeals of autobiography is that, when you read it, you can enter into another person's experience and discover what it feels like to be him or her.

In a similar way, when you write autobiography, you are made to think deeply about yourself and about how the events of your life have made you into the person that you are. There is no need to worry about how realistic your writing will be: you can be confident that your writing will be convincing, because you are writing from your own experience.

This unit introduces you to various kinds of autobiographical writing and will help you to develop your own ways of writing about yourself.

To carry out your work on this unit you will need to be with a partner or in a small group for discussion but when writing for your folder you should work alone. Try not to share your writing with others in your group until everyone has finished.

# Early memories

The best place to start is with your earliest memories. Here is an example taken from Shusha Guppy's account of her childhood in Persia (now Iran).

# THE BLINDFOLD HORSE

It is winter. A narrow, muddy street, flanked by low mud-brick walls beneath a cloudless steely sky. The ground rutted deep by cartwheels, pock-marked with mule and donkey hooves, covered with a thin layer of ice that crunches underfoot. Dirty patches of snow linger here and there at the base of walls. At the end of the street the embrasure of a door in front of which hangs an indigo-blue patched curtain, like a single spot of colour on a fawn canvas. From behind it comes a regular, monotonous muffled thud, like a distant hammer, followed by a whining screech.

This is my first memory – I must have been two or three years old. An inquisitive child, I stop and lift a corner of the curtain apprehensively: a pungent, spicy smell wafts across the street; inside is a small, dark room filled with clouds of yellow dust; in the middle, a huge circular stone with a mast at its centre is being dragged round and round by a large, emaciated horse on bending spindly legs. His eyes are blindfolded with a black cloth and, as he rotates the stone, a mustardy-yellow flour pours from under it into the surrounding gutter. The scene is lit by a single glass eye in the domed ceiling far above, which shoots a diagonal shaft of light and illuminates a column of dust whose yellow specks dance as if to the rhythm of the horse's hooves on the stony floor.

'Come along, child, we must hurry.' My mother. She takes me by the hand and pulls me away. I cling to the door, mesmerised, as the blindfold horse pulls round and round, its yoke screeching, its hooves thudding, its nostrils puffing jets of steam into the icy yellow air – turning, turning.

'Why are his eyes covered, Mother?'

'So that he doesn't see where he is, otherwise he would get dizzy going round in a circle all day, and he would balk. Blindfold, he can imagine he is walking in a straight line, in a field. But don't worry, at the end of the day they take off the cloth from his eyes and give him some lovely oats to eat. He is quite happy, really . . .'

The image dissolves.

But it comes back, leaping into memory at odd times – in daydreams or nightmares, in moments of doubt and anguish, and every time I use turmeric in cooking: the skeletal blindfold horse, chained to its treadmill in a dark room, going round and round, day after day, year after year, all the while imagining that he is galloping in a daisy-dotted prairie, for a bag of oats at the end of the day . . .

The blindfold horse, my earliest memory, *mon frère, mon semblable* . . .

*Shusha Guppy*

For Shusha Guppy, the Blindfold Horse has a special significance. It is a memory that returns; that will stay with her all her life.

# Group discussion

Examine closely the techniques Shusha Guppy uses to produce such an evocative piece of writing. In your group (a) list all the colours in the passage; (b) list all the sounds in the passage.

Now decide which are the most striking pieces of description. Choose two or three and indicate them by noting down the first words and the last words of each section. What makes them so powerful? Compare your choice with other groups. Did other groups pick the same images?

Why do you think that the author chose to write this episode in the present tense, i.e. *is* rather than *was*?

Why do you think that she feels this memory to be so important? What does the symbol of the blindfold horse tell us about the way she regards her childhood, adolescence and later life?

# Suggestion for writing

The best way to begin an autobiographical piece is to take a sheet of paper and make a list of memories. Do not try to start with the earliest. Instead, begin with your strongest memory and work backwards. As you get further back, you may find that your very early memories are only fragments, but write them down nonetheless. If you get really stuck, then talk to your family or look at some old photographs to jog your memory.

When you have filled your sheet with a number of hazy memories, decide which of them you are going to work on. One of them may obviously stand out but, if not, then pick two or three that seem promising.

Now take a separate sheet of paper and make a list of the colours and sounds associated with the memory. If you are working on more than one, then do this for each memory and use your lists to decide which one is the most vivid. From now on only work on this memory.

You now need to draft your writing. Write it out simply in the present tense. You may find this difficult at first because you are probably used to writing in the past tense, but you will find that it adds enormously to the immediacy of your writing – it will make you relive your memory. As you write, think of the shape of the piece – does it have a beginning, middle and end?

When you have finished your rough draft, bring the memory back into your mind. Run it through like a film from beginning to end. Are there details that stand out? Are there points during the memory when your feelings were particularly intense? If so, work on these passages in your writing. Your reader must be able to see what you saw and feel what you felt.

## *School*

Going to school is one of the most important of our early experiences and many writers have written brilliantly about their schooldays.

# *TROUBLE AT SCHOOL*

In the following extract from his autobiography *Beneath the Underdog*, Charles Mingus uses an unusual technique. He writes in the person of God looking down on the young Charles Mingus and commenting on his thoughts and feelings.

Mingus, who later became a great jazz composer and bass player, grew up in Watts, the black ghetto of Los Angeles. In the following extract he describes how he survived a very disturbing episode at school. As you read it, remember that Mingus is imagining the way God would describe events. He refers to the young Charles Mingus as 'My boy':

My boy was four years old and he felt pretty strange on his first day of school, clinging to Mama's hand, trotting along on his bow-legs, stumbling over his pigeon-toes, headed for the principal's office. Here went a brown baby with complexes, off to kindergarten to develop more. The kids all laughed as they passed and he didn't know if it was at him or his mother, who had taken off her work clothes and put on her Sunday go-to-meetin's for this occasion. He had overheard Daddy saying, 'Take that damned snuff out of your mouth! And don't dress so damn sloppy. You ain't fit for a pig to come home to!' It had to be true, Daddy was next to God and even sometimes told God what to do: 'God *damn* it!' he'd say when he got good and angry.

Weekdays Mama ploughed the back yard, planted the corn, tomatoes, string beans and onions, cleaned the chicken pens that held over a hundred hens and roosters, gathered eggs, mended the fence, cut and watered the grass, scrubbed and mopped the house, cooked and washed dishes, patched the children's clothes, made the girls' dresses and covered their ungodly asses with big black bloomers gathered with elastic just above the knee.

Were these strange little people really laughing at his mother? He thought she looked beautiful. He was confused by the yelling and fighting and screaming all round him but he hung on to her and didn't cry.

Mrs Corick, the big fat white lady principal was less than five feet tall and wore a short, neat little dress that flowered out to expose her legs, shaped like oversize country-fair blue-ribbon hams. She had bosoms like two strapped-down white winter melons. She looked bigger than a cow! Her face was fat like Santa's, bursting with joy, and she blushed continuously for no apparent reason. My boy wondered if she was rosy all over.

So Charles had entered school and his problems with the outside world began. I wanted him to know that he was not alone, that I was with him for a lifetime, so after this day I tried harder to communicate with him. It seemed difficult – maybe I had waited too long and he'd already developed a thinking pattern of his own.

One day he stole. He'd eaten his lunch on the way to school and at recess he went to the cloakroom and I saw him eating a sandwich that wasn't his. At noon another little kid began to cry and I looked closely at Charles's guilty face. I scolded him for that, and he heard. He promised he'd never take anything again as long as he lived.

It was about this time he heard himself called a strange name. Playing in the sandbox he was pouring nice hot sand down inside his pants because it felt so good. He was yanked from the box by a teacher. 'SEX PERVERT!' she said. He didn't know what it meant but he soon heard more on the subject. The little girl was Beulah Clemmons and Charles hadn't even noticed her that day, let alone looked up her dress. Besides, at home he'd seen his sisters in the bathtub and what could Beulah have under her dress different from Grace and Vivian? He was sitting on a bench at lunchtime, peeking around a corner of the schoolhouse, watching the girls and making eyes. Suddenly Mrs Pinkham, the spelling teacher, pulled him to his feet and slapped him and the Truant Officer grabbed him by the ear and booted him all the way up to the Fat Principal's office. 'Mrs Corick,' he said with satisfaction 'we caught him looking up Beulah Clemmons' dress! This boy should be sent to Boyle Heights this time for sure.' Boyle Heights was the school for disturbed and recalcitrant children.

'Mr Cuff, be good enough to go down and pick up Mrs Mingus,' the Fat Principal said. 'We're going to stop this kind of thing once and for all. You nasty thing, Charles!'

My boy remembered this was his Daddy's day off and began picturing his own funeral. Daddy was quick with the strap these days and often whipped him for things he hardly understood, like letting water get into his boots when he waded home from school in the flowing gutters after a heavy rain – though he was careful and never knew how it happened. Sometimes there were two thrashings, one from Mama's switch and the second, much worse, from Daddy's doubled-up strap.

He thought with terror of the punishment for wetting his bed. Daddy had warned him one night and the next morning Mama slipped in early and whispered, 'Get up, son, go pee – you don't want Daddy to beat you, you know what he said!' But she was too late and Charles began to cry. The bedroom door shot open and Daddy entered like the wrath of God. With his strap and fist he outdid himself while Charles was praying that Mrs Haynes next door would hear and yell as she always did, 'Stop abusing those children or I'll call the police!' But this time she must have been sound asleep.

The beatings at dawn went on for months and it go so sometimes they didn't even wake my boy. Daddy would beat on his body but the child was no longer inside, he was out with me waiting till the agony was over. He tried to find ways to foil these misguided parents, like changing the bottom sheet to the top, hoping it would dry with the heat of his body. Sometimes when Daddy thundered 'Did he wet?' Mama, the official pee-feeler, would reach under the blanket and touch the dampness of his long old-fashioned nightgown and, feeling sorry for Charles, she'd give his butt a little slap and say, 'I think he's going to be all right, Daddy.'

One morning my boy opened his eyes to see his father shaking a bottle under his nose. 'Good thing you didn't pee, boy! See this bottle of Lysol? Next time I'm gonna take this stuff and burn it right off!' The words struck icy horror to his heart and echoed through the years as he rose in the early hours and made an extra trip to the bathroom to relieve the damaged kidneys that had gone unattended in his childhood.

It was during this period that Charles asked me to take him away, out of himself, and let him die. When I refused, he no longer believed in me and began to pray to Jesus Christ to wake him up so his father wouldn't burn him or if that was impossible to take him up to heaven with the angels. So I began to watch over him all night and in the early morning I tugged at him and said, 'Wake up, Charles!' He jumped up blind with sleep and reached under the bed for the chamber pot. Once in his haste he mistook his shoe for the pot and gratefully made water in it while shouting 'Thank you, Jesus!' And so the morning beatings ceased and Charles was convinced Jesus had heard his cry for help. After that he called on Jesus for everything.

He was sending prayers up fearfully now as Mr Cuff and his parents entered the Fat Principal's office. His father looked straight at him and said, 'Now, son I don't want you to lie to me – if you do I'm through with you forever. This man here tells me you were looking up some girl's dress. I'm not going to whip you if you tell the truth. Where's the girl?'

'Here's Beulah,' Mrs Corick said.

'Did my boy try to look up your dress?'

'Yes. I was swinging on the rings and he was lying on the bench looking up my dress, that's what Mrs Pinkham said.'

'Son, why were you crying when I came in?'

'Mrs Pinkham was slapping me and –'

'Who the hell is Mrs Pinkham?'

'The spelling teacher.'

'What happened to your lip and your left eye?'

'Mr Cuff bumped me when he kicked me up the stairs.'

'I did no such thing!' said Mr Cuff.

'Yes, he did, the kids saw him,' Beulah said unexpectedly.

Mr Mingus took everyone outside to the scene of the crime. He had Beulah get up on the rings. Then he had the Truant Officer lie down on the bench, then the Fat Principal, and finally he lay there himself. He was getting madder by the minute and when he rose from the bench he said to Mr Cuff, 'Now, you red-necked son-of-a-bitch, tell me I'm a liar and kick my ass like you done my little boy 'cause you can't even see her from here, let alone see up her dress! You low trash, wasting my time bringing me down here! Lay a hand on my son again and I'll kick your ass all over this county of Watts!' Mama cried, 'Now Daddy, you know your temper! You've proven you're right. Let's be respectable and go home.'

*from* Beneath the Underdog *by Charles Mingus*

# Group discussion

- In the passage you have just read, Charles Mingus seems to be surrounded by hostility at school and at home. Look closely at the other people involved. They are:

| | |
|---|---|
| Beulah | The Truant Officer (Mr Cuff) |
| Mrs Pinkham | Mr Mingus |
| The Fat Principal (Mrs Corick) | Mrs Mingus |

In your group, discuss which of them seems the most hostile and which the most sympathetic to Charles. Take a piece of paper and write the names down in order, starting with the person closest to Charles and ending with the person most hostile to him.

When you have finished, compare your decisions with those of other groups. Is there general agreement?

• The passage contains two important episodes in Charles' life: the accusation of perversion and his parents' reaction to his bed-wetting. In your group discuss how you think Charles will develop after these events. Will they have a lasting effect on him? How will they influence his later life?

## Suggestions for writing

I Imagine each of the people involved in this episode in a situation in which he or she is describing to someone else what happened in the playground and the office:

Mr Mingus to a friend at work
Mrs Mingus to her mother
Beulah to a girlfriend
The Fat Principal to someone at the education office
Mr Cuff or Mrs Pinkham to another member of staff

Write two or three of these conversations. In each case try to achieve an authentic speaking style for the characters.

2 This episode in Mingus's life, coming as it does at a formative period, had an enormous influence on his adult life. Imagine that you are a psychiatrist who is treating the adult Mingus. He has just told you about these incidents. Write a report based on your understanding of what he has just told you under the following headings:

Relationship with father
Relationship with mother
Attitude to authority
Religious beliefs

Under each heading explain how the incidents are likely to have influenced Mingus's personality.

3 Charles Mingus writes through the eyes of God and so describes himself in the third person (he, Charles or my boy). You could use the same technique to write about your own school memories.

Either use Mingus's idea of God's view, or else simply write about yourself in the third person. It may seem odd at first but you will find that because it distances you from your earlier self you are able to write about things that might otherwise have been difficult to describe.

# I'VE CRACKED IT

Christopher Nolan suffered brain damage at birth and is severely disabled. Nevertheless, while still at school he published his first book, *Dam-Burst of Dreams*, to great critical acclaim. In his autobiography, *Under the Eye of the Clock*, he uses the name Joseph Meehan to represent his earlier self. In this extract he is desperate to make friends in a new class.

School students in Mount Temple were divided into a number of forms usually of mixed ability, boys and girls, and each form assumed a letter belonging to the word Dublin. Year by year the lettered classes changed pupils. Boys and girls had to change about in order to pursue different subjects. It so happened that Joseph's friends found themselves separated from their mate. It was September, the start of the school year, and Form 3L found Joseph on his own among a class of strangers. Everyone knew him – he was crippled gombeen-boy Joseph Meehan – but not bashful to the point of staying hidden, he now could claim genuine friends in school.

Form 3L offered a challenge to him. He now had to communicate with new boys and girls in this class. So he made his first move. He glanced hither and thither. He caught someone's eye, but they looked away. He caught someone else's eye and bowed his staccato bow at them, they gave him a hard look and then feigned interest in what Mr Casey was teaching. He tried again and again; boys and girls silently dismissed him. Schooling himself not to be easily offended, he didn't blame them – after all if he was in their shoes he'd likely act the same or even worse. Maybe he'd indicate his displeasure with a sneaky two-fingered sign! He chortled to himself and not heeding Jim Casey's explanation of assonance he tried again. Janey, I'm in luck, he mused as he caught the eye of the boy at the next desk. Joseph bowed at him and tried to smile naturally. The boy smiled briefly and looked away. Then he seemed to have second thoughts and looking hard and questioningly he smiled again, and leaning over towards Joseph he rested his elbow on the arm of the wheelchair and whispered, 'Hi. I'm Paul Browne. Are none of your set in this class?' Joseph shook his head. 'Don't worry about being on your own,' said the new classmate. 'I'll be beside you and I'll look after you.' Joseph nearly exploded with delight. Jim Casey was standing there teaching about assonance, while under his nose real live drama was damn well in the making. Seeing but a whispering duo the teacher made no comment, after all how could he have imagined the significance of the scenario. Right there in front of him sat an able-bodied, voice-gifted youth volunteering to be a friend to a mute crippled boy.

Paul straightened up and began to turn his attention to what the teacher was saying, while Joseph sat viewing the sky outside the high window. Gulls swept back and forward in the framed picture, but he now joined them and scrambling on golden wings he mentally yelled in competition with the scavengers. I've cracked it, he yelled, I've bloodywell cracked it. Then swinging his mind back to reality, he realized that the class was nearly over and his ear had not trapped one word of Jim Casey's assonance. But anointing hope was flowing over the young student. He was amazed by Paul's boldness of approach, but time was going to prove that not only could Paul converse with his new friend but mute crippled Joseph could TALK back.

As school life daily herded him in flock formation, he silently framed questions that he wanted to put to his classmates. He pondered on the entreaties he'd like to make. His questions would test their shrewdness. He listed them: will you accept that boy's blood courses in my veins, that boy's thoughts cram my skull, boy's ambitions crowd my mind, that normal consciousness beats alongside yours? Then as though helping them he hinted: but unlike all of you, I am celibated by dank felons of armour-harnessing. He mentally moded the questions, but to his amazement his valiant friends began to frame those selfsame questions and even more wonderfully they now boldly made their observations known to him and to each other. 'Jaysus Joseph you must be damn-well driven mad by your spasms,' they said. 'Do you wish you were just like us? ... Do you get awful fed up listening to kids smart-arsing about you and the eejit you are with your arms movin'? ... Do you ever wish you could give them a boot in the arse and say "f— off ya bleedin' prig"?' How Joseph would react to their observations would lead them to make wider observations about girls, sex, bastardization of all sorts, about adults and their old-fashioned hang-ups. Joseph revelled in their coarseness – they voiced his bloody frustrations, they gave comfort by seeking to get inside his frame and their cursing his condition brought laughter bubbling to his now. Sassy rasps of schoolboy's humour cast comfort mantle-like around Joseph and friendship cabled a denim lifeline between him and his mates.

*from* Under the Eye of the Clock *by Christopher Nolan*

## Group discussion

Perhaps because of the extreme nature of his disabilities (he has to type using a device attached to his forehead), Christopher Nolan has developed a very distinctive style. You may have noticed the short sentences and unusual vocabulary. These strange constructions are often brought into play when he is describing his own predicament. In the third paragraph on p. 12, for instance, he says 'I am celibated by dank felons of armour-harnessing.' What do you make of this description? In your group, discuss what you think Christopher is trying to express here.

During his schooldays, Christopher Nolan never talks about anyone teasing him because of his disabilities. Indeed, he is often surprised at how wonderful his friends can be and nearly all of his school memories are pleasant. The sudden recognition of friendship in this passage is a good example of this.

## Suggestion for writing

Many people experience their most important and lasting friendships at school. The beginning of a friendship is often marked by a small occurrence; someone you like chooses to sit next to you or you are asked to join in a game. Think about these important moments in your own school life. You could write, like Christopher Nolan, using an invented name or you could tell the story simply in the first person.

# JACKIE'S STORY

Some children find adjusting to the demands of school too much to cope with. They soon begin to truant, which leads them into conflict with teachers, parents and, eventually, the law.

In 1982, Centerprise, a community publisher in Hackney, London, received a package containing two hand-written exercise books. They contained 'Jackie's Story', the anonymous autobiography of a long-term truant.

As you will see from the following extract, 'Jackie' writes candidly about her truancy in a straightforward, powerful style.

It all began when I started my secondary school. I hadn't minded the primary school much, it was alright, I had lots of friends there and we had a laugh but this place felt different. For a start they gave us all a load of tests all the first week. Apart from that the first week was alright, everyone was new and no-one knew their way about. The second week though I pretended to my mum I was sick and she let me stay at home for the Thursday and Friday. When I got back it felt really funny walking in there and I felt I didn't belong there. Everyone seemed to know what they were doing. I stayed that day but the rest of the week I acted sick again amd my mum let me stay off, looking after my two twin sisters who were three and my brother who was four, nearly five and would start school after Easter.

It was really good going to the park with them or playing in the house if my mum wasn't cleaning. I preferred it to going to school but in the evenings I went out and mucked about with all my friends who lived round the estate. A few of them went to my new school and they didn't dislike it too much. When the next Monday came round I asked my mum if I could stay off but she said I'd get into trouble if I did, so I went in the morning, it was really awful; none of my old friends were in my class and so when we had PE, I pretended to have forgotten my kit so I wouldn't have to do it with no-one to muck about with. The teacher made some sarky remark and I swore at her, I hadn't really thought it just slipped out, she said I had to go to the detention room or something but I went out of school.

I went to the shopping centre until dinner time then I went in to get my afternoon mark then I went home. My mum seemed surprised to see me but she didn't ask any questions and the next morning when I came down to breakfast in my normal clothes instead of my uniform she just said she had some shopping for me to do. My dad got home later that day, he was a lorry driver and was on the road for days at a time, he wanted to know what I was doing home. When he heard why he walloped me and then he was going to wallop my mum too but there was a ring at the door. The teacher who came into the house stayed for about half an hour and when she left said she'd hope to see me the next day. My dad said 'You can bloody rely on it, she'll be there.' The teacher had wanted to know why I had been to school so irregularly and when I said I didn't like it she said I hadn't even tried it.

The next morning I felt really sick but my dad made sure I got to school by walking all the way with me. When I got there a teacher thanked him for coming and said she was glad I had come. After registration I was going to go out but there was a teacher by the main gate and she asked me what I was doing. I muttered something and walked back to the building. First thing we had Maths and when I went into the room, a bit late, the teacher looked up. I was expecting a rude remark but all he said was he was glad I'd come and to sit down. I didn't understand most of the lesson but it wasn't too bad except when he started asking everyone to go up and do a sum, I was nerving myself to refuse but didn't have to as he missed me out. Next we had PE and I lost courage and hid in the toilets all lesson. The next lesson was English which I thought would be good, I was disappointed when she handed out poetry books, I'd thought we could write stories. At dinner time after I'd eaten my dinner there was nothing to do so I walked round the shopping centre not far from the school. I was going to skip off in the afternoon but the thought of my dad made me go back. The afternoon was alright but I was glad when the pips went and we could all go.

When I got home my dad was out and my mum asked me how it was. I said it was alright and she seemed relieved. I went solidly for two weeks except for PE lessons, I either pretended I'd forgotten my stuff or I went to the medical room or I stayed in the toilets. After two weeks my dad went off again for two weeks. That was really great because it meant he'd be away the

next week and half-term which was the following week. I had
the next week off, my mum phoned in to say I had flu. We
didn't mention it to my dad when he came back. The first day
back after half-term was awful as I'd had two weeks off. I went
in for registration, then having learned my lesson, waited a bit
before leaving through the gate, it was worth it as there was
no-one there.

All that week I managed that trick without being caught. The
next week my dad was away so I stayed at home. The third
week after half-term when my dad was at home (I stayed at a
friend's house instead of going to school) there was a phone call
one evening. Thankfully I got there first and changing my
voice I said that 'my daughter' had measles. The teacher on the
other end sounded suspicious and said she'd like to see my
parents as it was a week and a half since I'd been in school – the
school had obviously been fooled by my register trick. I thought
up an excuse and said that 'my daughter' would be back at
school the following Monday. On Sunday night I forged a note
from my dad and took it in the next morning. The head of my
year called me on the tannoy and when I went into her room
there was another lady sitting there too. I sat down and the year
head – Mrs Halse said that the other lady was an Educational
Welfare Officer, I looked blank and she explained that the lady
was responsible for seeing people came to school regularly. I
began to feel scared. Mrs Halse said I'd been less than half the
time I should have done and the term wasn't even over yet.
They asked me about my family and what I liked and didn't like
about the school. I tried to pretend I quite liked the place to
shut them up but I don't think they were taken in. The most
terrible thing was that Mrs Halse said she thought I should be
put 'on report' for a while. That meant I had a card that all the
teachers had to sign to say I'd attended their lesson. She said,
frowning, that some teachers said they hadn't seen me for a
month or more. I didn't say anything, I had a feeling she
wanted me to admit to something but as she had no proof I
kept quiet. For that week I went to every lesson, even PE. The
next two weeks though my dad was away and I stayed at home
with my mum and brother and sisters.

Half-way through the second week the EWO – Miss Aldrich
came round and wanted to know why I was off school. I was
surprised to see her. My mum said I was ill but I don't think
Miss Aldrich was even half convinced that was the truth. She

said my parents would have to go to court if I didn't go to school and at the thought of what my dad would say my mum said she'd see I did. I went back the next day and had to carry the stupid report card about again. The next week my dad was still away so I went in one day then missed a day and repeated that all week. No-one came round so I could stay at home in peace.

The next week when my dad came home a letter arrived asking him and my mum to go and see the headmistress. My dad wanted to know what it was all about and he and my mum had a flaming row and then he went out and got drunk. He did that only very rarely. I wasn't invited to go with them but when they got back I heard all about it. The headmistress had suggested I go to another school unless I was prepared to go to that one all the time. My dad had lost his temper my mum said and had said they weren't giving me a chance. The headmistress had then threatened to have my parents taken to court if I missed another day without a doctor's note and my dad had walked out leaving my mum to say she'd sort something out.

When Monday arrived my mum and dad had a row because my dad said he wanted me to stay off, whether I wanted to go or not to 'Teach them sods a lesson', as he said. My mum didn't want any trouble though and said for once I should go. I felt a bit of a traitor but I agreed with my dad and said I wasn't going. It was nice staying away and not causing trouble for my mum because apart from the first row, she said it was alright and I went to the park with my sisters. I stayed off all that week and the next while my dad was away; he told us if anything happened to let him know. Nothing did and I thought stupidly that they'd given up and I could stay away all the time now.

When I'd been away from school four weeks, a letter came saying my parents had to go to court. My dad was away so my mum went by herself. When she got back she said if I didn't go they'd fine my parents a hundred pounds. She said I had to either go to that school or another one. I said I'd keep at the one I was at as I thought going to another school wouldn't make any difference. The following Monday I went to school. Mrs Halse met me at the gate and said I'd have to go back on report. I felt really funny going into lessons with people I hadn't seen for more than a month but no-one said anything about me.

All that week I went in, to my mum's delight. My dad said he'd get the doctor to write a note if I wanted to stay away the next week. I don't know why he suddenly changed his mind about me staying off, he can't have hated the headmistress that much. The next week was just like old times, all of us at home. After that week it was the Christmas holidays – three weeks off without anyone coming round. When it was time to go back I didn't. I expected my mum to object but she didn't. The second week of term I went on Monday and Mrs Halse wanted to know where I'd been. I said I'd been ill but I saw she was going to tell Mrs Aldrich. I stayed away the rest of the week and to my surprise Mrs Aldrich didn't come round or phone. I stayed off until half-term, I got quite a pattern to the day. I always got up late, that was one of the things I hated about going to school – early rising.

After half-term my mum said I should go in for a day or two 'Just to let them know you're alive' as she put it. I went in on Monday and they didn't even give me a report card so I bunked off PE and no-one said anything. I thought it was odd no-one even said anything but found out last lesson that Mrs Halse for once was away, it was my lucky day. The next day my mum said I could stay off so I did. I went in on Friday and as Mrs Halse was still off, I went home after dinner.

It was nearly a week later that Mrs Aldrich came round and talked to me and my mum, my dad was out. She asked me what I did at home and in the evenings. I didn't go out in the evenings much anymore. She asked me when I'd be twelve and I told her – April the 27th. Then she asked me if I'd mind her talking to my mum on her own so I went away. When she'd gone my mum said they wanted me to go to a truancy centre. I asked her what for but she didn't seem to know, only that the court said I had to go somewhere. I asked when I had to start and she said the following Monday.

*from* Jackie's Story *(anon)*

# Group discussion

'Jackie' never explains what it is that she so dislikes about school. Discuss what it is that you think causes her to truant. Here are some questions to help you focus your discussion:

(a) Do you feel that the school is in any way to blame?

(b) Does 'Jackie's' home life contribute to her increased truanting?

(c) What sort of a person do you feel 'Jackie' to be?

Remember to keep going back to the extract for evidence.

## Suggestions for writing

1 'Jackie's Story' would make a good play. 'Jackie' tells us her story in a very unsensational way but underneath her plain prose there is obviously a drama unfolding. Use this extract as the raw material for a play about truanting. Try to stick to 'Jackie's Story' as much as possible but if you feel that your play would benefit, then you can add in episodes either from your own experience or from your imagination.

2 Ask your teacher or librarian for a copy of *The Friends* by Rosa Guy. It is a very popular book and should be easy to get hold of. It tells the story of a girl newly arrived in America from the Caribbean. The early chapters deal with her experiences of school and her attempts to adjust to the demands it makes on her.

Compare this fictional report with the autobiographical account by 'Jackie'. You could also bring in your own experiences and those of your friends and call your essay 'Coming to terms with school'.

3 Do you think teachers are sufficiently aware of the difficulties that some children face in adjusting to school? Discuss how you think teachers could increase their understanding of these problems. Again, use your own experience if it is appropriate. You may wish to interview teachers (particularly those involved in the induction of first year pupils in your school) to find out how they deal with children who are having problems.

# Early learning

It is often the case that our experiences as children have a profound effect on our later adult life. Many great scientists and artists attribute their careers to the influence of a particular event in their childhood or to a relationship with an influential adult.

Of the three writers in this section, the first, Christy Brown, became an award-winning writer and artist. The other two, Primo Levi and Richard Feynman, became important scientists who never lost their childhood sense of wonder and, unlike many scientists, always endeavoured to explain their work to the public.

# THE LETTER 'A'

Christy Brown was born the victim of cerebral palsy, only able to control the movement of his left foot. It was not until he was four months old that his mother noticed that there was something wrong with the way he held his head and took him to see a succession of doctors. Each doctor declared that he was mentally defective and a hopeless case. His mother refused to accept this and continued to believe that inside the crippled body was a working brain. She treated him in the same way as her other children, talking to him and providing him with stimulation. Despite the constant warnings of her family not to raise false hopes, she continued in this way for years until, as this passage from Brown's autobiography *My Left Foot* shows, all her labours finally bore fruit.

I was now five, and still I showed no real sign of intelligence. I showed no apparent interest in things except with my toes – more especially those of my left foot. Although my natural habits were clean I could not aid myself, but in this respect my father took care of me. I used to lie on my back all the time in the kitchen or, on bright warm days, out in the garden, a little bundle of crooked muscles and twisted nerves, surrounded by a family that loved me and hoped for me and that made me part of their own warmth and humanity. I was lonely, imprisoned in a world of my own, unable to communicate with others, cut off, separated from them as though a glass wall stood between my existence and theirs, thrusting me beyond the sphere of their lives and activities. I longed to run about and play with the rest, but I was unable to break loose from my bondage.

Then, suddenly, it happened! In a moment everything was changed, my future life moulded into a definite shape, my mother's faith in me rewarded and her secret fear changed into open triumph.

It happened so quickly, so simply after all the years of waiting and uncertainty that I can see and feel the whole scene as if it had happened last week. It was the afternoon of a cold, grey December day. The streets outside glistened with snow; the white sparkling flakes stuck and melted on the window-panes and hung on the boughs of the trees like molten silver. The wind howled dismally, whipping up little whirling columns of snow that rose and fell at every fresh gust. And over all, the dull, murky sky stretched like a dark canopy, a vast infinity of greyness.

Inside, all the family were gathered round the big kitchen fire that lit up the little room with a warm glow and made giant shadows dance on the walls and ceiling.

In a corner Mona and Paddy were sitting huddled together, a few torn school primers before them. They were writing down little sums on to an old chipped slate, using a bright piece of yellow chalk. I was close to them, propped up by a few pillows against the wall, watching.

It was the chalk that attracted me so much. It was a long, slender stick of vivid yellow. I had never seen anything like it before, and it showed up so well against the black surface of the slate that I was fascinated by it as much as if it had been a stick of gold.

Suddenly I wanted desperately to do what my sister was doing. Then – without thinking or knowing exactly what I was doing, I reached out and took the stick of chalk out of my sister's hand – *with my left foot.*

I do not know why I used my left foot to do this. It is a puzzle to many people as well as to myself, for, although I had displayed a curious interest in my toes at an early age, I had never attempted before this to use either of my feet in any way. They could have been as useless to me as were my hands. That day, however, my left foot, apparently on its own volition, reached out and very impolitely took the chalk out of my sister's hand.

I held it tightly between my toes, and, acting on an impulse, made a wild sort of scribble with it on the slate. Next moment I stopped, a bit dazed, surprised, looking down at the stick of yellow chalk stuck between my toes, not knowing what to do with it next, hardly knowing how it got there. Then I looked up and became aware that everyone had stopped talking and were staring at me silently. Nobody stirred. Mona, her black curls framing her chubby little face, stared at me with great big eyes and open mouth. Across the open hearth, his face lit by flames, sat my father, leaning forward, hands outspread on his knees, his shoulders tense. I felt the sweat break out on my forehead.

My mother came in from the pantry with a steaming pot in her hand. She stopped midway between the table and the fire, feeling the tension flowing through the room. She followed their stare and saw me, in the corner. Her eyes looked from my face down to my foot, with the chalk gripped between my toes. She put down the pot.

Then she crossed over to me and knelt down beside me, as she had done so many times before.

'I'll show you what to do with it, Chris,' she said, very slowly and in a queer, jerky way, her face flushed as if with some inner excitement.

Taking another piece of chalk from Mona, she hesitated, then very deliberately drew, on the floor in front of me, *the single letter 'A'*.

'Copy that,' she said, looking steadily at me. 'Copy it, Christy.'

I couldn't.

I looked about me, looked around at the faces that were turned towards me, tense, excited faces that were at that moment frozen, immobile, eager, waiting for a miracle in their midst.

The stillness was profound. The room was full of flame and shadow that danced before my eyes and lulled my taut nerves into a sort of waking sleep. I could hear the sound of the water-tap dripping in the pantry, the loud ticking of the clock on the mantelshelf, and the soft hiss and crackle of the logs on the open hearth.

I tried again. I put out my foot and made a wild jerking stab with the chalk which produced a very crooked line and nothing more. Mother held the slate steady for me.

'Try again, Chris,' she whispered in my ear. 'Again.'

I did. I stiffened my body and put my left foot out again, for the third time. I drew one side of the letter. I drew half the other side. Then the stick of chalk broke and I was left with a stump. I wanted to fling it away and give up. Then I felt my mother's hand on my shoulder. I tried once more. Out went my foot. I shook, I sweated and strained every muscle. My hands were so tightly clenched that my fingernails bit into the flesh. I set my teeth so hard that I nearly pierced my lower lip. Everything in the room swam till the faces around me were mere patches of white. But – I drew it – *the letter 'A'*. There it was on the floor before me. Shaky, with awkward, wobbly sides and a very uneven centre line. But it *was* the letter 'A'. I looked up. I saw my mother's face for a moment, tears on her cheeks. Then my father stooped down and hoisted me on to his shoulder.

I had done it! I had started – the thing that was to give my mind its chance of expressing itself. True, I couldn't speak with my lips, but now I would speak through something more lasting than spoken words – written words.

That one letter, scrawled on the floor with a broken bit of yellow chalk gripped between my toes, was my road to a new world, my key to mental freedom. It was to provide a source of relaxation to the tense, taut thing that was me which panted for expression behind a twisted mouth.

*from* My Left Foot *by Christy Brown*

# THE LETTER 'A' (screenplay)

*My Left Foot* has now been made into a film. In order to do this, Shane Connaughton and Jim Sheridan (the director) wrote a screenplay. This is written in the form of a play with extensive 'stage directions' explaining the action (written in the present tense). This is how the same episode appears in the screenplay:

INT. CHRISTY'S HOUSE. NIGHT
*Everybody is sitting around.* MR BROWN *is sitting reading the paper in bad humour. The children are doing their homework.* CHRISTY *is sitting there with the chalk between his toes. He has drawn a straight line. Hold on:* CHRISTY's *foot as he makes another line at a 45-degree angle to the first.*
SHEILA: Look at Christy, Mammy, He's making a triangle.
    (CHRISTY *finishes the line, looks at everybody looking at him and then raises his foot to finish the figure. He starts halfway up one of the lines.*)
MR BROWN: He's starting in the wrong place.
    (CHRISTY *tries to join the two lines together, but his foot gives*

*up and it ends in a squiggle. Then* MR BROWN *takes the chalk*
*in his hand. He draws a triangle.*)

Look, Christy, that's a triangle.

(CHRISTY *looks at him furiously. Rubs out his father's line.*)

MRS BROWN: It's not a triangle, it's an A.

(CHRISTY *grunts a deep strong grunt of acknowledgement.*
*There is something primitive and territorial about it. It is his*
*first articulation in the film. The father eyes him warily, sits back*
*and looks at* MRS BROWN. *All the kids are watching* CHRISTY.
TOM *comes through the door.*)

TOM: What's up?

MR BROWN: Keep quiet.

TOM (*Slight threat*) All I said was 'What's up?'

MR BROWN: And all I said was 'Keep quiet.'

(*He starts to take off his belt.*)

TOM: (*Standing*) All I said was . . .

(*The father lets out a primal roar.*)

MR BROWN: Sit down.

(TOM *sits, mesmerized and slightly embarrassed. Close on:*
CHRISTY *as he watches the tribal war.* MRS BROWN *rushes from*
*the room and comes back with some money in her hand.*)

MRS BROWN: Here.

MR BROWN: What's that?

MRS BROWN: Money. Go and have a drink.

MR BROWN: Where did you get it?

MRS BROWN: From the fairies. Go and get a drink for
yourself.

MR BROWN: I don't need a drink. I just need to be obeyed in
my own home.

(CHRISTY *has picked up the chalk again and is drawing on the*
*floor again. They all watch him. He again draws the beginning*
*of a triangle or an A. He stops when he completes two sides.*)

MRS BROWN: Go on, Christy.

(CHRISTY *starts at the outside of the second lines and draws*
*another line back up at an angle of 45 degrees.*)

MR BROWN: If that's a f—ing A, I'm Adolf Hitler.

(*At the top* CHRISTY *starts back down.*)

SHARON: He's drawing another triangle.

(CHRISTY *finishes the line. They all watch him.*)

MRS BROWN: Than's an M.

(*Another deep primitive grunt from* CHRISTY. *He immediately*
*starts on another letter. Close on: his face, and you would think he*
*was having a baby as the sweat stands out on his brow. He draws*

*a curious half-moon and then goes on to make a primitive O.)*

O.
*(Nobody is able to talk. All have been dumbstruck by* CHRISTY.
*He continues drawing on the floor and there is a magical effect
to the lettering, almost as if he were discovering the letters, as if
they were his own shapes newly thought up, a strange alphabet
springing from a deep urge to communicate. He makes the T.*
MR BROWN *is transfixed and mouths the word* MOT. CHRISTY
*continues on and does the letter H. All the children during the
time* CHRISTY *is drawing have edged towards the mother.
Involuntarily the younger ones have put their arms around her
legs.* MR BROWN *stands alone, unaware in the drama that he
has become isolated. When* CHRISTY *draws the E, one of the
kids says 'Mother', but* MRS BROWN *stops her with a raised
finger, afraid that any break in the silence will destroy the
magic. The perspiration on* CHRISTY'S *brow is translucent. He
continues drawing the R with a maniacal energy. When he
finishes he looks at the father, defiance, anger and ten years'
frustration released in a minute.* MR BROWN *is stunned;* MRS
BROWN *and all the children wait on his reaction.* MRS BROWN
*appears calm and assured, an interior knowledge made flesh.)*
MR BROWN: Good Jesus, holy Jesus, suffering Jesus. (*Picks*
CHRISTY *up.)* You're a Brown all right.
Christy's a Brown. (*holds him aloft like a chalice.*)
Christy f—ing Brown. Give me that money, woman.
(MRS BROWN *gives him the money.)*

*from the screenplay of* My Left Foot *by
Shane Connaughton and Jim Sheridan*

## Group discussion

- Why do you think the following changes have been made to the original?

  (a) In the screenplay, 'Sheila' represents all Christy's sisters and 'Tom' represents all his brothers.

  (b) In his autobiography, Christy describes how he wrote the word 'Mother' some months after being taught the alphabet by his mother. The screenplay, however, incorporates the event into this scene.

- Examine the screenplay carefully (remember the directions in italics are as important as the dialogue) and compare it with the original piece of autobiography. Here are some questions to help you with your discussion:

(a) How is Mr Brown portrayed in the screenplay? Do we get the same impression from Christy's autobiography?

(b) How do the extracts establish the following relationships: Christy and his mother; Christy and his father; Mr Brown and Mrs Brown?

(c) The screenplay shows a great deal of tension within the family. How is this indicated? Is this tension present in the auto-biography?

(d) In which version do we learn more about Christy? Mrs Brown? Mr Brown? the family? the room?

## Suggestions for writing

I Use the ideas that came out of your discussion of the two extracts to write a comparison of the autobiography and the screenplay in which you discuss the way that character, emotion and atmosphere are portrayed in each version.

2 Christy's struggle is only a more intense version of the struggle we all face when we attempt to acquire new skills. Can you remember the feelings of frustration and elation when you first learned to ride a bike, for instance, or use roller skates? Write about how it happened.

If you enjoyed reading this extract, there is another piece from 'My Left Foot' on p. 47.

# TADPOLES

In the following extract, Primo Levi, a scientist, describes a summer spent in the valleys of Piedmont when he was a young boy. His fascination with nature leads him to examine tadpoles more closely.

Our summer holiday lasted the whole length of the school vacation: about three months. Preparations began early, usually on St Joseph's Day (the nineteenth of March): since we weren't rich enough to afford a hotel, my parents would tour the still snow-clad valleys of Piedmont looking for lodgings to rent – preferably somewhere served by the railway and not too far from Turin. We didn't have a car (this was the early thirties, and almost no one did) and for my father, who hated the sultriness of summer anyway, time off was restricted to three days around the August bank holiday. So, just to sleep with the family and in the cool, he would subject himself to the drudgery of a twice-daily train journey out to Torre Pellice or Meana, or any of the other modest villages within a hundred or so kilometres of the city. For our part we went every evening to the station to wait for him. At daybreak he set out again, even on Saturdays, to be in the office by eight.

My mother began the packing around the middle of June. Apart from bags and suitcases, the main load consisted of three wicker trunks, which when full must each have weighed at least two hundredweight; the removal men came and hoisted them miraculously onto their backs and carried them downstairs sweating and cursing. The trunks contained everything: bed-clothes, pots and pans, toys, books, provisions, winter and summer clothing, shoes, medicines, utensils – as if we were departing for the Antipodes. Usually we arranged our destination together with other families – relations or friends; it was less lonely like that. In this way we took a part of our city along with us.

The three months went by slowly, and quietly, and dully, and punctuated by the abominable sadism of Holiday Homework: a contradiction in terms! My father spent only Sundays with us, and those in his own fashion. He was a thorough-going urbanite: the countryside did not agree with him. He disliked the emptiness of the fields, the steepness of the paths, the silence, the flies, the discomforts. The mornings he would spend reading, taciturn and cross; in the afternoon he dragged us off for an ice-cream at the only café in the village, and then he would retire to play the tarot with the miller and his wife. But for my sister and me the months in the country meant a regularly-renewed union with nature: humble plants and flowers whose names it was fun to learn in Italian and dialect; the birds, each with their own song; insects; spiders. On one occasion in the wash-basin, a leech, no less, graceful in its swimming, undulating as if in a dance. Another time, a bat that zigzagged dementedly about the bedroom, or a stone-marten glimpsed in the twilight, or a mole-cricket, a monstrous, obese little insect, neither mole nor cricket, repugnant and menacing. In the courtyard garden well-disciplined tribes of ants rushed about their business, and it was enthralling to observe their cunning and their stubborn stupidity. They were held up as an example in our schoolbooks: 'Go to the ant, thou sluggard; consider her ways, and be wise' (Proverbs, 6:6). They never took summer holidays. Yes, they may have been virtuous little creatures, but it was the obligatory virtue of prisoners.

The stream was the most interesting place of all. My mother took us down every morning to sunbathe and to paddle in the clear, clean water, while she got on with her knitting in the shade of a willow. You could wade the stream safely from bank to bank, and it was a haven to creatures the like of which we had never seen. On the river-bed black insects staggered along resembling huge ants, each one dragging behind it a cylindrical case made of tiny pebbles or little pieces of vegetation, into which it had threaded its abdomen; only its head and claws poked out. When disturbed, the creatures recoiled like a shot into their little mobile homes.

In mid-air hovered wondrous dragonflies, frozen in flight, iridescent in metallic turquoise; even their buzzing was metallic, mechanical, bellicose. They were miniature war machines, dropping in one stroke, dart-like, on some invisible prey. On the dry, sandy banks green beetles ran nimbly to and fro; the conical traps of the antlion sprang open. Such ambushes we witnessed with a secret sense of complicity, and hence of guilt, to the extent that my sister, overwhelmed every so often with pity, would use a twig to divert some poor ant on the point of a sudden and cruel death.

Alongside the left bank the water teemed with tadpoles in their thousands. Why only on the left? After much fruitless discussion about sun and shade we noticed that along that side ran a footpath much used by anglers; the trout were wise to this, and kept to the safety of the right bank. Accordingly, to avoid the trout, the tadpoles had established themselves on the left. They aroused conflicting feelings: laughter and tenderness – like puppies, new-born babies and all creatures whose heads seem too big for their bodies – and indignation, because every so often they ate each other. They were chimaeras, impossible creations, yet they sailed along swiftly and surely, propelling themselves with elegant flicks of the tail. Between head and tail they had no body, and this was what seemed incomprehensible and monstrous; all the same, the head had eyes and a mouth – a voracious mouth curiously down-turned as if sulking – ever in search of food. We brought a dozen back home and put them, to my mother's disapproval, in the portable 'camping' bidet, slung on its trestle – we had covered the bottom with sand from the bed of the stream. The tadpoles seemed at home there, and sure enough after a few days they began their metamorphosis. This was a novel spectacle, as full of mystery as a birth or a death – enough to make us forget our holiday homework, and for the days to seem fleeting and the nights interminable.

Every morning, indeed, had a surprise in store. The tail of one tadpole began to thicken, close to its root, into a small knot. The knot enlarged, and in two or three days out pushed a pair of webbed feet – but the little creature made no use of them: it let them hang limp, and carried on waggling its tail. A few more days, and a pustule formed on one side of its head; this swelled up, then burst like an abscess, and out came a fore-limb already perfectly formed, minute, transparent – a tiny glass hand, already treading water. A little later, and the same happened to the other side, while the tail was already starting to shrink.

This was a dramatic time: one could see that at a glance. It was a harsh and brutal puberty: the tiny creatures began to fret, as if an inner sense had forewarned them of the torment in store for those who change their shape, and they were confounded in mind and body: perhaps they no longer knew who they were. Their swimming was frantic and bewildered, their tails growing ever shorter and their four legs still too weak to use. They circled around in search of something – air for their new lungs, perhaps, or maybe a landing-place from which to set forth into the world. I realized that the sides of the bidet were too steep for the tadpoles to climb out, as was clearly their wish, and so I positioned in the water two or three small wooden ramps.

It was the right idea, and some of the tadpoles took advantage of it – but could you still call them tadpoles? Not any more: the larvae had gone; now there were brown frogs as big as beans – but frogs with two arms and two legs, folk like us, who swam breast-stroke with difficulty but in the correct style. And they no longer ate each other, so we felt differently towards them, like a mother and father: in some way they were our children, even if our part in their metamorphosis had been more of a hindrance than a help. I sat one in the palm of my hand: it had an ugly mug, but a face nevertheless; it looked at me, winked, and its mouth gaped open. Was it gasping for air, or was it trying to tell me something? Another time it set off determinedly along my finger, as if along a springboard. The next instant it was gone, with one senseless hop into the void.

Bringing up tadpoles, then, was not so easy. Only a few of them cottoned on to our little safety-ramps and got out onto dry land. The rest, already deprived of the gills provided for their aquatic infancy, we would find in the morning, drowned, worn out by too much swimming, just like a human swimmer trapped inside a lock. And even those who had understood the purpose of the landing-stage, the more intelligent ones, did not always live long. The tadpoles responded to a perfectly natural instinct – the same instinct that has driven us to the moon, that is epitomized in the commandment, 'Multiply and replenish the earth' – which spurred them to forsake the stretch of water where they had completed their metamorphosis. It did not matter whither – anywhere else but there. In the wild, for every likely pool, for every bend in the stream, there will be another not far away, or perhaps a damp meadow or a marsh. Thus some do survive, by migrating and colonizing new surroundings. Still, even in the most favourable conditions a large proportion of these neo-frogs are bound to die. And it is for this reason that the mother frog exhausts herself laying interminable strings of eggs: she 'knows' that the infant mortality rate will be breathtakingly high, and she allows for this as our country forebears did.

Our surviving tadpoles dispersed around the courtyard garden in search of water that wasn't there. We tried to keep track of them through the grass and the gravel. The boldest, labouring to cross the granite pavement in clumsy hops, was spotted by a robin, who made a quick meal of him. And that very instant the white kitten, our gentle little playmate, who had watched all this transfixed, took a prodigious leap and pounced on the bird, whose mind was still on its lucky catch. She half-killed it, as cats do, and took it off into a corner to toy with its agony.

*Primo Levi*
*(Translated from the Italian by Simon Rees)*

## Group discussion

- Split 'Tadpoles' into sections (no more than six). In your group, give each section a title that reflects its most important theme. When you have decided on your sub-titles, compare them with those of other groups. Have you decided on the same section breaks? Do you all agree on the themes of each section?

- Here are some statements about the passage. Decide which you agree with and which you do not.

  (a) In the passage nature is seen as cruel and ugly

  (b) The passage is about growing up

  (c) Primo Levi learns something from his experience of bringing up tadpoles

  (d) Primo is unlike his father

  (e) The children were wrong to tamper with nature

When you have discussed the statements and come to your decisions, compare them with those of other groups. Do you all agree? Is there anything in his childhood behaviour to suggest that Levi would later be a scientist?

## Suggestions for writing

1 Imagine that this passage represents an important episode in Primo Levi's autobiography and that a film is going to be made of it. Of

course, these events will only take a few minutes in the film and so will have to be reduced to six important scenes. Each scene does not need to be described in detail but, taken together, they must tell the whole story, so choose them carefully.

If you turn to page 23 of this unit you will see an extract from the screenplay of *My Left Foot*, the film of Christy Brown's autobiography. This example is rather long, most film scenes are much shorter and often they will contain no dialogue. For instance:

INT. LIVING ROOM. DAY

MRS BROWN *is polishing shoes. There are six pairs of children's and Mr Brown's boots. She polishes away as* CHRISTY *watches her, especially when she holds her back in pain.*

Notice that the scene starts with a note of where and when it takes place, beginning with either INT. for interior or EXT. for exterior. The characters who feature in the scene are always printed in capital letters to differentiate them from characters who are only mentioned.

Your six scenes from 'Tadpoles' should use the same format as these extracts from the screenplay of *My Left Foot*.

You may add dialogue of your own into the scenes if you think it will make them more effective.

2  Primo Levi's experiment with the tadpoles forces him to realise that death is part of nature. He doesn't say how he felt about watching his kitten half kill th, robin but many people have been shocked when faced with the ugly side of nature.

Read the poem 'Death of a Naturalist' by Seamus Heaney (available in *Poetry Workshop*, ed. Michael and Peter Benton, Hodder and Stoughton). Compare Levi's description of his childhood experience with Heaney's poetic version of a childhood encounter with tadpoles. What are the similarities and differences?

In your writing, go into the detail of how both writers evoke the images and feelings of their childhood.

3  As very young children we are often shown animals portrayed as if they were humans (in cartoons on TV or as characters in picture books, for example). It can come as a great shock to find out how animals really behave in the wild. You may have had experiences yourself in which you were shocked or revolted by the behaviour or

appearance of animals. Write about your experiences explaining how you felt at the time.

OR

You may feel that it is our own fault if we react in this way. Many people are fascinated by animals and, through their experience of caring for them, come to accept behaviour that others would find revolting (the way that cats will bring in 'presents' of dead mice, for instance, or the fact that snakes must be fed live food). Write about your own experience of animals and what it is that attracts you to your favourite animal.

You could follow this by compiling a small booklet or pamphlet in which you give details of how to look after your particular pet. Begin by collecting information under headings such as 'Housing', 'Feeding', etc. and then start to plan the layout of the booklet. Remember, it must be easily understood by people who have very little experience of keeping animals.

(If this subject particularly interests you then turn to Unit Six, part of which deals with animals and the question of their rights.)

# THE MAKING OF A SCIENTIST

In this extract from his memoirs, Richard Feynman remembers his relationship with his father and how he believes it made him into a scientist.

Feynman didn't actually write this himself. The piece is a transcription of a conversation that he had with Ralph Leighton. As you read it, you will hear Feynman's voice in the writing just as if he were sitting next to you and talking to you – try to work out what it is about the writing that tells you that it is a transcription of someone speaking.

Before I was born, my father told my mother, 'If it's a boy, he's going to be a scientist.'* When I was just a little kid, very small in a highchair, my father brought home a lot of little bathroom

---

*Richard's younger sister, Joan, has a PhD in physics, in spite of this preconception that only boys are destined to be scientists.

tiles – seconds – of different colors. We played with them, my father setting them up vertically on my highchair like dominoes, and I would push one end so they would all go down.

Then after a while, I'd help set them up. Pretty soon, we're setting them up in a more complicated way: two white tiles and a blue tile, two white tiles and a blue tile, and so on. When my mother saw that she said, 'Leave the poor child alone. If he wants to put a blue tile, let him put a blue tile.'

But my father said, 'No, I want to show him what patterns are like and how interesting they are. It's a kind of elementary mathematics.' So he started very early to tell me about the world and how interesting it is.

We had the *Encyclopaedia Britannica* at home. When I was a small boy he used to sit me on his lap and read to me from the *Britannica*. We would be reading, say, about dinosaurs. It would be talking about the *Tyrannosaurus rex*, and it would say something like, 'This dinosaur is twenty-five feet high and its head is six feet across.'

My father would stop reading and say, 'Now, let's see what that means. That would mean that if he stood in our front yard, he would be tall enough to put his head through our window up here.' (We were on the second floor.) 'But his head would be too wide to fit in the window.' Everything he read to me he would translate as best he could into some reality.

It was very exciting and very, very interesting to think there were animals of such magnitude – and that they all died out, and that nobody knew why. I wasn't frightened that there would be one coming in my window as a consequence of this. But I learned from my father to translate: everything I read I try to figure out what it really means, what it's really saying.

We used to go to the Catskill Mountains, a place where people from New York City would go in the summer. The fathers would all return to New York to work during the week, and come back only for the weekend. On weekends, my father would take me for walks in the woods and he'd tell me about interesting things that were going on in the woods. When the other mothers saw this, they thought it was wonderful and that the other fathers should take their sons for walks. They tried to work on them but they didn't get anywhere at first. They wanted my father to take all the kids, but he didn't want to because he had a special relationship with me. So it ended up that the other fathers had to take their children for walks the next weekend.

The next Monday, when the fathers were all back at work, we kids were playing in a field. One kid says to me, 'See that bird? What kind of bird is that?'

I said, 'I haven't the slightest idea what kind of a bird it is.'

He says, 'It's a brown-throated thrush. Your father doesn't teach you anything!'

But it was the opposite. He had already taught me: 'See that bird?' he says. 'It's a Spencer's warbler.' (I knew he didn't know the real name.) 'Well, in Italian, it's a *Chutto Lapittida*. In Portuguese, it's a *Bom da Peida*. In Chinese, it's a *Chung-long-tah*, and in Japanese, it's a *Katano Tekeda*. You can know the name of that bird in all the languages of the world, but when you're finished, you'll know absolutely nothing whatever about the bird. You'll only know about humans in different places, and what they call the bird. So let's look at the bird and see what it's *doing* – that's what counts.' (I learned very early the difference between knowing the name of something and knowing something.)

He said, 'For example, look: the bird pecks at its feathers all the time. See it walking around, pecking at its feathers?'

'Yeah.'

He says, 'Why do you think birds peck at their feathers?'

I said, 'Well, maybe they mess up their feathers when they fly, so they're pecking them in order to straighten them out.'

'All right,' he says. 'If that were the case, then they would peck a lot just after they've been flying. Then, after they've been on the ground a while, they wouldn't peck so much any more – you know what I mean?'

'Yeah.'

He says, 'Let's look and see if they peck more just after they land.'

It wasn't hard to tell: there was not much difference between the birds that had been walking around a bit and those that had just landed. So I said, 'I give up. Why does a bird peck at its feathers?'

'Because there are lice bothering it,' he says. 'The lice eat flakes of protein that come off its feathers.'

He continued, 'Each louse has some waxy stuff on its legs, and little mites eat that. The mites don't digest it perfectly, so they emit from their rear ends a sugar-like material, in which bacteria grow.'

Finally he says, 'So you see, everywhere there's a source of food, there's *some* form of life that finds it.'

Now, I knew that it may not have been exactly a louse, that it might not be exactly true that the louse's legs have mites. That story was probably incorrect in *detail*, but what he was telling me was right in *principle*.

Another time, when I was older, he picked a leaf off a tree. This leaf had a flaw, a thing we never look at much. The leaf was sort of deteriorated; it had a little brown line in the shape of a C, starting somewhere in the middle of the leaf and going out in a curl to the edge.

'Look at this brown line,' he says. 'It's narrow at the beginning and it's wider as it goes to the edge. What this is, is a fly – a blue fly with yellow eyes and green wings has come and laid an egg on this leaf. Then, when the egg hatches into a maggot (a caterpillar-like thing), it spends its whole life eating this leaf – that's where it gets its food. As it eats along, it leaves behind this brown trail of eaten leaf. As the maggot grows, the trail grows wider until he's grown to full size at the end of the leaf, where he turns into a fly – a blue fly with yellow eyes and green wings – who flies away and lays an egg on another leaf.'

Again, I knew that the details weren't precisely correct – it could have even been a beetle – but the idea that he was trying to explain to me was the amusing part of life: the whole thing is just reproduction. No matter how complicated the business is, the main point is to do it again!

Not having experience with many fathers, I didn't realize how remarkable he was. How did he learn the deep principles of science and the love of it, what's behind it, and why it's worth doing? I never really asked him, because I just assumed that those were things that fathers knew.

My father taught me to notice things. One day, I was playing with an 'express wagon,' a little wagon with a railing around it.

It had a ball in it, and when I pulled the wagon, I noticed something about the way the ball moved. I went to my father and said, 'Say, Pop, I noticed something. When I pull the wagon, the ball rolls to the back of the wagon. And when I'm pulling it along and I suddenly stop, the ball rolls to the front of the wagon. Why is that?'

'That, nobody knows,' he said. 'The general principle is that things which are moving tend to keep on moving, and things which are standing still tend to stand still, unless you push them hard. This tendency is called "inertia", but nobody knows why it's true.' Now, that's a deep understanding. He didn't just give me the name.

He went on to say, 'If you look from the side, you'll see that it's the back of the wagon that you're pulling against the ball, and the ball stands still. As a matter of fact, from the friction it starts to move forward a little bit in relation to the ground. It doesn't move back.'

I ran back to the little wagon and set the ball up again and pulled the wagon. Looking sideways, I saw that indeed he was right. Relative to the sidewalk, it moved forward a little bit.

That's the way I was educated by my father, with those kinds of examples and discussions: no pressure – just lovely, interesting discussions. It has motivated me for the rest of my life, and makes me interested in *all* the sciences. (It just happens I do physics better.)

I've been caught, so to speak – like someone who was given something wonderful when he was a child, and he's always looking for it again. I'm always looking, like a child, for the wonders I know I'm going to find – maybe not every time, but every once in a while.

*from* What Do You Care What Other People Think
*by Richard Feynman*

## Group discussion

- Why do you think Feynman's father had this effect on him? In your group, discuss what it is that his father does to arouse the boy's interest in science.

- Many children are fascinated by science either through school, parents or other adults. Is anyone in your group really keen on science? How did their interest come about?

- Science teachers in secondary school often complain when students say that they find their subject boring. After all, the teacher no doubt feels that all scientific enquiry is fascinating. Why do you think so many young people find science difficult in secondary schools? Is there anything in Feynman's experience that you think science teachers could learn from?

## Suggestions for writing

1 In a sense, Feynman's father is his teacher. His 'lessons' are relevant and interesting. Can you remember a lesson that you particularly enjoyed? It could be a lesson in which you suddenly found that you understood something properly for the first time or were intro-duced to something that you found particularly fascinating. Write about how it happened and how you felt at the time.

2 Do you remember being taught something by your parents or another adult; knitting, carpentry, sewing or car maintenance, for instance? How did they go about teaching you? Did you pick it up quickly or were you hopeless to start with? Tell the story of how you learned.

3 Feynman chose to write his book by talking to a friend and taping the conversation. The tape was then transcribed. Many people find that they are able to talk about their experiences more easily than they could write about them. You could try this for yourself by telling some of your favourite memories to a friend or one of your family and taping it. Transcribing a tape-recording can take a long time and needs enormous concentration but often the results are worth it. You may find that you have created a fresh and amusing piece of writing.

OR

You could interview an older person about his or her childhood memories. You may find that you will need to prompt your interviewee with questions, so prepare some beforehand.

# Extensions

Now that you have reached the end of the unit, here are some ideas to help you evaluate what you have read and written and some sugges-tions of ways to extend your work.

1 Look back over your writing. Which piece do you feel is most successful? Does your teacher agree? If there is one piece that stands out from the others, is it worth adding to it or improving it in any way?

Do you want to connect two or three of your pieces together so as to make your own autobiography? You may need to fill in the gaps so that the writing covers your life adequately.

(If you want to read some autobiographies written by school students, then have a look at *Our Lives* published by The English Centre.)

2 Is there one extract that you enjoyed reading more than the others? If so, you might like to read the whole book from which it came. The books used in this unit are:

*The Blindfold Horse* by Shusha Guppy (Heinemann, 1988)
*Beneath the Underdog* by Charles Mingus (Weidenfeld & Nicolson, 1971)
*Under The Eye of the Clock* by Christopher Nolan (Weidenfeld & Nicolson, 1987)
*Jackie's Story* (Centerprise, 1984)
*My Left Foot* by Christy Brown (Secker and Warburg, 1954)
*My Left Foot* screenplay by Shane Connaughton and Jim Sheridan (Faber and Faber, 1989)
*What Do You Care What Other People Think* by Richard Feynman (Unwin Hyman, 1988)
Primo Levi's 'Tadpoles' was taken from the magazine *GRANTA*.

3 You could combine a study of two of these books together to make an interesting open study or project. For example, Christy Brown and Christopher Nolan both write about growing up severely disabled. Do they suffer the same kinds of emotional and social deprivation? Do they struggle against, and conquer, the same kind of prejudice?

4 Read 'Jackie's Story', which is available in its complete form from Centerprise, 136 Kingsland High Street, London E8, and compare it with *Rhino*, a play by David Leland (Cambridge University Press). Both deal powerfully with the pressures that cause young people to truant from school and the well-meaning but often misguided attempts to help them.

# 2 FIRST LOVE

Our first physical relationship with someone is an important event in our lives. It may not last very long but, because it is such an emotional experience, it is likely to remain a vivid memory. The first time, after all, can never be repeated.

In this section, three writers recall their early attempts at sexual relationships.

The first piece by Stephanie Calman is a lighthearted account of that all-important first kiss.

# A KISS BEFORE LYING

There is something very special about the first boyfriend in your life. I'm not thinking of the first man you sleep with or fall in love with, but the first one who ever asks you out on a date. He may not have been gorgeous; he may have been spotty and not washed his hair too often, but for him in your history there will always be a significant place. He was the first person of the opposite sex who showed enough interest to buy you a hamburger or a cinema ticket. He was also probably the one with whom you learned to kiss.

In all the discussion about sex that goes on, kissing tends to get overlooked, which is a pity. The assumption seems to be that once people start using their sex organs full time, they don't need to think about communicating mouth to mouth. Yet kissing is a very worthwhile activity whose contribution to peace in the bedroom shouldn't be underestimated. Not only can it be therapeutic and relaxing, it even has some advantages over sex. It requires less space and privacy, being a convenient and rewarding pastime for cars, cinemas, lifts, aeroplanes, park benches, street corners, stationery cupboards and the edges of armchairs; the absence of great expectations makes disappointment unlikely, and there is no known record of anyone having got pregnant from a kiss.

Like sex, though, kissing is a method of expression which can teach you a lot about a man. It is a lip signature which can be executed with or without sensitivity, clumsily, urgently, languidly or in a boring, self-absorbed way. Everyone has their own style. Some men take considerable care over it; some don't.

And this matters. There's an enormous difference between a man who takes his time and varies the pace spontaneously, and one who just shoves his tongue in and out for twenty seconds and that's it.

I don't know whether upbringing has anything to do with it, but it is interesting that while some men kiss very neatly, almost fastidiously, without leaving a molecule of dribble, others make quite a mess. You know who I mean – the ice-cream eaters who open their mouths as wide as they can, and simultaneously kiss the whole area from your nose down to your chin. They make no attempt to hit the mouth specifically, just aim in the general direction of your face. The last time I had one of these, I thought I was going to drown. My face was awash, and some of it had gone up my nose. Not having a lifejacket, I had to improvise safety measures, using what materials came to hand. First, unsuckering his mouth – the presence of a vacuum made this difficult – I turned my head to one side so that my face was against his chest. Then I pretended to nuzzle. And all the time he thought I was nuzzling, I was wiping the spit off on his shirt. I know it sounds horrible, but it was his spit.

Though individual styles of kissing may differ like sexual techniques, one cannot be relied upon to give an accurate indication of the other. In one person the two may bear no resemblance at all. In the case of Peter, I was positively misled. He was one of the great kissers of his time. To him it wasn't a prelude, but a whole concert, a creation worthy of reviews. And it wasn't just what he did with his lips: he had a way of putting his hands around the back of my neck that made me think my spine was going to explode. Kissing him was so good that afterwards I felt like lying back and smoking a cigarette. I should have done. When we did get into bed, it was such a non-event – I can't tell you. The experience was honestly so null it failed to impress itself sufficiently upon my memory for me to describe it to you. Basically that was the way the evening ended: not with a bang but a wimp.

I'm not blaming him – entirely. I just wonder where the magic had gone. Perhaps it all got used up in the kissing. Afterwards what I really wanted to do was carry on seeing him, starting with entering the bar or restaurant, and finishing just before we would have had sex. But you can't do that. It seems it has to be all or nothing, lovers or friends. You can't have something hybrid in between.

It was this that made me long, albeit briefly, to be a teenager again. When you're a teenager you don't have to commit yourself to one side of the fence or the other. You can spend a lot of time kissing. You can have relationships that consist almost entirely of kissing and nothing else. I kissed a boy called Larry for a large part of 1974.

Larry became my first proper boyfriend the night he took me to Dalston Odeon to see – or not to see – *Thunderbolt and Lightfoot*, starring Clint Eastwood. Larry was not gorgeous. He wore unglamorous black-rimmed glasses and an anorak which reached to his knees. Also, he was not thin. But he impressed me for two quite valid reasons: 1, his attitude towards me did not constitute total indifference, and 2, he talked expansively of one day going to America and owning a car.

I came bounding into school to tell my best friend Kathy, who was engaged in writing 'Mike' with different coloured pens all over her desk. She was not won over even by the fact that he was fifteen. She considered the matter, and with the clarity of judgement absent in those hidebound by etiquette, said: 'He's fat.'

Nevertheless, while Clint Eastwood flickered superfluously in the distance, Larry put his arm around my shoulders, pulling me towards him, and I held my breath. It was agony. The suspense of not knowing when he was going to kiss me was unbearable. Also, the arm of the seat was digging into my ribs. Eventually he hauled me even further over the divide and turned my head to face his. His lips came, but there was something awful with them, like a shellfish without the shell. I had no idea what was going on. Nowadays there are books to teach you about these things; at thirteen I was still reading comic stories about girl detectives and kidnapped hockey teams. In the darkness I pressed my lips together more firmly, sure that I was party to something really terrible and perverse. Next to my ear Larry's voice hissed a reprimand: 'Stephanie!'

'What?'

'You're supposed to open your mouth.'

It would be a few years before I heard that exhortation again.

I brought Larry home to meet my mother one evening after school. This, luckily, was not too nerve-racking an experience, as I was more fortunate in the mother department than some.

A girl in my class called Emily had a mother who liked to ask boys questions when they came round. Not being of the view that young people could make choices and operate relationships under their own steam (or God forbid, under each other), she would interrogate potential companions and later inform Emily which she should choose. This had tragic consequences for Emily. After school her house was like *Mastermind*, only by the time they'd answered the questions, nobody wanted the prize.

My mother offered Larry something to eat. She always offered visitors something to eat, no matter what time of day or night, believing that allowing people to leave without their stomachs registering 'full' was tantamount to turning them starving into the street.

Larry said: 'A cheese sandwich, please.'

Mother offered, but making the sandwich was my job. Outside mealtimes, all family members were supposed to serve their own guests, and that left me facing the cheese. This was bordering on the feeble, and it certainly wasn't Larry's problem, but I had a horror of cheese. I hated eating, touching or even looking at the stuff. It's still true of the eating: I could be cured of anything by aversion therapy if instead of electric shocks they gave me cheese. Even so, in front of this precious boyfriend I was determined not to lose face. I dragged my sister into the kitchen by her comic and begged her to make the sandwich for me. She agreed, but there was a price.

'It'll cost you,' she said, with the expression of a loan shark regarding a man who has asked for another day's grace.

'What? What? Anything. Hurry up.'

'The dressing-table with the four moving drawers from your dolls' house.'

'Oh, no! All right then. But not the stool.'

'The stool goes with it, as you very well know.'

While Larry ate his sandwich – little guessing at what price – mother asked him: 'And what is your ambition?'

'I'd like to have my own harem,' he said.

In the bedroom with the lights off, Larry and I practised kissing. It took us a long time getting it right. Eventually we found a mode we liked and went over it a lot. Apart from the cinema, there was rarely a change of location. We gave up practising at Larry's house, because he had an Italian grand-mother who sat in a room at the back of the ground floor, listening for girls. Apparently if she ever heard more than two feet going up the stairs – unless it was Larry's parents, and even they couldn't be too obvious – terrible punishments would ensue. We never found out the nature of these punishments, but then we never had time to do anything wicked. It took us nearly a whole afternoon just to get up the stairs. Once we had crept, shoeless, out of earshot and into his room, Larry would put on his record player, one of those old automatics with an extra arm that could play the same record (or three) over and over again forever until you pulled out the plug or shot yourself. To the accompaniment of Led Zeppelin, for hours continuously, we would kiss. By six o'clock on the fifth occasion I had heard 'Stairway to Heaven' 124 times. I nearly went down to the grandmother and gave myself in.

So, sick of crawling up Larry's stairs in balaclavas and boot black, we transferred the sessions permanently to my house. Here the consequences of discovery were less diastrous, and the figure to be avoided not a grandmother but a ten-year-old sister with a developing business head.

'What were you doing in there with Larry?' she asked me one evening, looking like someone eager for the means by which to acquire more dolls' house furniture.

'He was helping me with my French homework,' I said, inwardly congratulating myself on such inspiration at short notice. Yet she did look suspicious. Raising one eyebrow, she skipped away, her eyes glistening with visions of a dolls' house decorated like Versailles.

*from* Dressing for Breakfast *by Stephanie Calman*

## Suggestions for writing

Now that you have read Stephanie Calman's account of her early love life you could try writing your own humorous pieces. You could base your writing on your own experience but you don't have to. Here are some ideas.

1 Think about the episode in the cinema with Larry. You could base your story on this common experience – the first date in the back row of the cinema. You could tell it from either point of view or you could even write two versions of the episode; one told by the girl and one told by the boy.

2 When you introduce your new boy or girlfriend to your parents, things can sometimes get embarrassing. Write about a first meeting of this kind. You could write it from any point of view (even the parents'!). Again, you could write more than one version of the occasion from different points of view.

3 Younger brothers or sisters can often be a nuisance when you are trying to appear cool in front of your new boy/girlfriend, but imagine how they view the whole business. You could write from their point of view as they watch the goings-on with bemusement.

# A LOOK OF PITY

This is another extract from Christy Brown's autobiography *My Left Foot*, the story of how a severely disabled boy struggles towards self-expression. In stark contrast to Stephanie Calman's lighthearted account of everyday adolescence, this piece delves deeply into the feelings of a young boy who must come to terms with the fact that he can never be like the others.

She lived a few doors away from my house. She was small, energetic, gay, with a mass of brown curls framing her pretty elfin face with its lively green eyes and pouting lips. Unfortunately Jenny was a coquette; she could start a riot among all the boys on our street by just using those lovely eyes of hers in the right way. They were all crazy about her and there were many fights when they started arguing about who would marry her when they grew up into men.

I didn't go out any more, but that didn't stop me from seeing Jenny. I worshipped her from afar, that is from my bedroom window. It made me lazy in my painting, for whenever I heard Jenny's voice in the street below I'd crawl over to the window and sit on the bed, gazing out at her as she ran and skipped about with the other girls, whom I didn't notice at all. One day she looked up at me as I sat gazing down on her. I felt my face grow hot and made to draw back, but at that moment she smiled. I managed to smile back, and then she threw me a kiss. I could hardly believe my eyes when she did this, but she did it again before running away down the street, her dark curls flying and her white dress blowing in the wind.

That night I tore a page from an old jotter and, holding the pencil in my shaking toes, I wrote a passionate little note to Jenny, which I got one of my younger brothers to deliver, threatening him with my foot if he didn't give it to Jenny herself. I told her in the note that I thought she was the prettiest kid on our street and that I'd paint her lots of pictures if she'd let me. Then, in a hurried postscript, I told her that I loved her 'lots and lots of times'.

I waited for my brother to come back in excitement and fear, not daring to hope that Jenny would reply. In a half an hour's time he returned – with a note from her tucked up his jersey!

I took the note and read it eagerly, quite forgetful of my brother, who stood by staring at me in a funny way as if he thought I'd gone mad or something. I read Jenny's little letter over and over again, especially the part where she said she'd come and see me in my back yard the next day if I wanted her to. There was a queer fluttering inside me and a lightness in my head. I felt myself go hot and cold in turn. After a while I looked up. My brother was still standing with his hands behind his back and his mouth open, a look of bewilderment in his big blue eyes as he fixed them on my face. I yelled at him to 'scram', and he scuttled from the room like a startled rabbit. Then I threw myself back on the pillow and sighed, my heart jumping crazily.

I kept the appointment next day, all spruce and 'done up' with Tony's de luxe hair grease actually dripping down my fore-head. Little Jenny was very sweet. We sat and looked over some of my paintings, and she gave a little gasp of admiration at each one I showed her. I was shy and awkward at first because of my slurred speech and the way I used my foot instead of my hands. But Jenny was either a very innocent person or a very tactful one, for she didn't seem to notice anything queer about me, but talked on gaily to me about games and parties and the boy next door the same as if I had been Peter or Paddy. I liked her for that.

We became great pals, Jenny and I. We never said a great deal to each other, but we exchanged innumerable little notes each week and she'd steal over to see me every Saturday night, bringing me little books and magazines which I never read but which I treasured very much, storing them all away in the old worm-eaten cupboard in my bedroom.

I was secretly proud that I, a cripple, had made friends with the prettiest and most sought-after girl in our neighbourhood. I often heard Peter saying fervently that Jenny was a 'peach' and that he'd do anything to be her favourite 'beau'. Every time I heard this I felt very proud of myself and enormously vain, thinking myself quite a conqueror, because it was not I who went to Jenny, but Jenny who came to me!

Peter became suspicious and one Saturday he came upon Jenny and me as we sat together in the back yard, our heads very close to one another, although we were only looking at some old story book that Jenny had brought along. I got red in the face, but Jenny didn't move. She just lifted her head, smiled at my brother briefly, and bent over the book again. Peter gave me a murderous look and went into the house, banging the door after him.

That evening, before she left, Jenny sat very quietly, toying idly with the book, a little frown creasing her forehead and her lower lip pushed out, as she always looked when she wanted to say something difficult. After a little while she got up, hesitated, then suddenly knelt down on the grass beside me and kissed me very tenderly on the forehead. I drew back, surprised, bewildered, for she had never kissed me before.

I opened my mouth to try and say something, but at that moment Jenny sprang to her feet, her face flushed and her eyes wet with tears, and rushed from the garden, her small black shoes clattering noisily as she ran down the stone path and disappeared into the street.

She didn't come for weeks after this, and I didn't hear from her although I fairly bombarded her with notes. In the meantime Peter tried to discourage me by telling me many wicked tales about poor little Jenny, but I didn't believe him a bit, not even when he told me that she made every one of the boys pay her a penny for every kiss she gave them.

'That's why I'm always broke!' he said mournfully, his hands stuck in his empty pockets.

I often sat up in my bed at night, thinking of Jenny and the way she kissed me that day in the back garden. I felt very melancholy and alone. Why doesn't she come, I asked myself, as I tossed restlessly in the dark, hearing Peter snoring comfortably at my side.

My fourteenth birthday came along, and among the other birthday cards I got that morning there was one written in a small childish hand which was Jenny's: but still she never came to see me. I often saw her from my bedroom window playing in the streets below, but she kept her eyes away from my house and never looked up once. I'd sit at the window for hours, hoping she'd glance up at me, until the twilight came and everything grew dark and I could see nothing more save the dim whiteness of her frock as she ran along the street with the other girls, while a laughing crowd of boys chased after them.

To hide my disappointment I painted furiously for the whole of every day, painting crazy little pictures that had neither pattern or theme. They were just haphazard slices of my boiling mind dashed on to the paper wildly and recklessly.

Then one day as I sat disconsolately in the back yard with my back against a soapbox I heard a step close by. I looked up wearily.... It was *Jenny*! She stood a few feet away, at the entrance to the yard, her slim, childish figure outlined against the white wall behind her, vividly bright in the June sunshine, her shadow falling crookedly on the warm concrete ground. She was looking across at me, but – it was with a *look of pity.*

I knew then, as I came to know many times later, how bitter and crushing a simple look of pity can be to someone like myself who needs something other than sympathy – the strength that only genuine human affection can give to the weakest heart.

I lowered my head under her pitying gaze and without a word being said on either side Jenny turned slowly and left me to myself in the yard.

I became different after that. For a few blissful weeks I had allowed myself to dream that I was a normal, ordinary boy of fourteen who thought himself 'in love' with the sweetest girl in the whole neighbourhood and who was foolish enough and vain enough to think that she cared for him in return. Now all that make-believe was at an end, but the bitterest of all was the realisation, that I had tricked myself into believing that my affliction didn't matter, that my 'queerness' was merely self-consciousness which nobody else took any notice of. I saw now what an ass I had been to fool myself so magnificently.

*from* My Left Foot *by Christy Brown*

Examine carefully the way that Jenny is presented in the extract. Do we feel any sympathy for her? What motivates her to act in the way that she does?

# Suggestions for writing

1 Write a version of 'A Look of Pity' from Jenny's point of view. How might her friends regard her relationship with Christy? Why does she choose to befriend him and why eventually does she stop seeing him?

2 In many ways Stephanie Calman's 'A Kiss before Lying' represents the world that Christy Brown can never inhabit.

 Both books describe attempts to come to terms with sexual feelings but one is written by a crippled boy, the other by an able-bodied girl; one is serious, the other humorous. Write a comparison of 'A Look of Pity' and 'A Kiss before Lying'.

3 Christy Brown describes the tremendous feeling of excitement before the first date – 'I felt myself go hot and cold in turn.' Write your own description of the experience of a first date. It could be entirely fictional or you could base it on your own experience. If it is fictional, though, make sure that it is as realistic as you can make it.

# THE GOLDEN TIME

Sally Brampton recalls a time of death as well as love one summer in the park.

I fall in love in the summer. Not every summer, for I have not had as many loves as I have had summers. And nor would I want them. That would prove a careless nature and I would not want you to think that of me. Or them. I have loved both men and women. And they have loved me back. I left them, all of them, in the winter. Or perhaps they left me, seeing that the one they loved was no longer, had faded with the light. November is my bitterest month.

I first fell in love in June. Completely, utterly, irredeemably in love. I was hopeless with it. The sun was shining. I wore blue; blue the pale colour of the sky on a fine morning. It was the day my grandfather died.

They told me he was dead. I was furious with him. He wanted to die. I wanted him to live. I watched the cracks appear in his

shabby waistcoat with its faded leather buttons and darned patches. He could not mend it. He mended everything else. All his books were faded to the colour of dried blood, the carboard covers held together with great black stitches, the spines cobbled to the covers with coarse button thread. He laboured over them daily, outlined their titles in thick blue biro. They were the ugliest books I ever saw.

My grandfather hated garlic and abroad, liked sugar on everything including lettuce, loved my grandmother. They would sit and hold hands in front of me in front of the television. He once came up behind her as we were talking and absent-mindedly clasped her breasts in his hands. He smiled at the look on my face. I thought they were very old. He thought I was very young.

He lived for two years after she died. For two long, hot summers he sat by the blazing gas fire, the television turned on full volume. There was a shrine of photographs of her in one corner of the room. He let no one in; he wanted nobody. The family had to beg to be allowed in. He was as helpless, and hopeless, as a child without her. He only looked after his books. The biro titles were inches thick.

He called me and asked me to visit him. He gave me her old silver; mismatched knives and forks and spoons. He said that he had had enough, was bored without her. I was too young to believe him. He smiled kindly at me and kissed me goodbye. He was taken into hospital with suspected pneumonia. They gave him a cardiogram. He was fine. The next day his heart stopped.

I thought love had killed him. I went out, through the hot metallic streets and bought a bottle of wine. The city was stunned by heat, people stumbled along the pavements like sleepwalkers, car engines buzzed like insects. I took the wine out to the garden and lay on the grass, the sun hot on my face, the wine cool in my mouth and watched the fat bumblebees loop around the wedgewood delphiniums in happy, drunken turns. I sang as I drank as I lay there. I sang Tiptoe Through The Tulips, the song he had sung when first he met me and danced me round the room as I balanced with my toes on his shiny brown leather shoes. I was four years old. I thought he was the most glamorous thing I had ever seen. He had eyes the colour of cornflowers but sparkly like the sea on a summer's day.

I fell asleep and dreamed that he was happy, that his old eyes were shiny blue again. I woke in the shadows. The sky had deepened to cerulean. The roses looked plump and pink and sleepy. I felt thin and pale and wanted the night to grieve in. But the sun still shone gold on the houses and I was late.

I had promised to go and see a man I had met only once before. He was glamorous too, in a crumpled sort of way and his eyes were kind even though they were the colour of autumn. He seemed to like me, although quite why he did confused me. I would have given him quite a different sort of woman.

I telephoned him to cancel – although I did not know it at the time – my first love. Perhaps my grandfather was looking over me, for the years after were cruel. I told him that I was too sad to go out and play. He told me to take a taxi, that he would pay the other end, that he would look after me. I thought that that was kind and I was young and poor enough to think that taxis were exciting. I took the bus.

It was a gorgeous evening. The world looked young. Everybody smiled at the light. People strolled through the streets with no particular place to go; the men with their jackets slung over one shoulder, shirt sleeves rolled up, ties stuffed in their trouser pockets while the women swayed and fluttered in their light, bright cotton frocks. Some walked barefoot in the park while others lay on the grass, the women with their faces turned into their lovers' shoulders. That year it seemed as if the summer could never end, as if the autumn could not snatch the leaves from the trees, the winter suck the heat from the ground.

I sat on the bus and watched the light fade on Piccadilly, blur the hard edges of the buildings, sweep the dust from the pavements. The air was heavy with the smell of sun-baked tar and concrete, sweet with the scent of new-cut grass. He was waiting for me on the corner, his hand full of coins to pay the taxi. He laughed to see me walk down the street and told me that I looked like the morning, dressed as I was in blue. He gave me a whisky, for shock he said. I had never drunk it before and I liked it very much.

We went for a walk in the park. He walked with his hand held at the nape of my neck. I wanted to touch him but did not dare. He told me repeatedly that I was wonderful, which I thought extraordinary. I was not used to people who spoke so frankly. He asked me if I had missed him. I said that I had not even thought about it, and that made him laugh. But I knew that if I never saw him again, I would miss him very much.

There was a woman in the park with her dog, an alsatian. She wore a checked tweed coat of two shades of brown. It flared like an A, and had large, round horn buttons and a raggedy fur collar. On her feet were new, blue carpet slippers, and she wore no stockings. Her hair was parted in the centre with a childish, short, bluntly cut fringe, and was pulled back in a pony tail. Her face was very old. Her dog ran in wide circles around her, watching all the time to see that she didn't stray too far. She spoke to him sternly, but with love. Apparently she went to the park every day. She was always alone but for her dog who never went and played with other dogs or chased the birds, but stayed by her side. She never changed her coat, no matter what the weather.

We went to a restaurant in Soho and sat at a table by a window which opened right up, so we seemed to be sitting on the street. The tablecloths were pale pink and there was a deep pink rose on the table in a bright little ceramic jug. He gave it to me and said that they were his favourite roses. It smelled like pepper. I had never met a man who liked flowers before. We ate a salad with seafood in it and spaghetti with a sauce called pesto. The smell of petrol fumes from the cars going past made the food taste like metal. It was delicious.

He had eyes that crinkled permanently at the corners and dark hair that was silvered at the temples, although he was not old. The first time we made love, he shook. I was amazed that anyone would shake for me. In the mornings he would run my bath and scent it with rose geranium oil. The bathroom was white and pale blue and always filled with sunshine. I would sit in the bath and watch the brilliant blue patch of sky through the sloping attic window.

I spent every afternoon in the park. I was gold, that summer, tanned by the sun and warmed to the bone with him. The dog woman was there every day. We never spoke or smiled but sometimes she nodded imperceptibly to show that I belonged. In the evenings I would lie and wait for him in the grass, watching for his slow, familiar walk. He would come to me and, putting his hand at the nape of my neck, would tilt my head and bury his face in the curve of my neck and shoulder. He said I smelled like summer.

He left in September. I went with him to the airport and he pulled me to him as he sat on the orange plastic chair and he buried his head between my breasts to breathe the smell of me. He told me he was proud because I had not cried. I wept. He sent me roses every Monday, pink and smelling of peppers, and wrote to me every day.

One morning in November, when the sky was grey and grumpy with rain, he telephoned to tell me that it was too hard. He said that he could not live with his heart in one city and his head in another. I mourned for two years. The sky was not blue the next summer, nor the next.

That was many years ago and I have since had summers, and I have had love. But sometimes I go and sit in the park. The woman and her dog are still there. She has not changed her coat. The last time I saw her she smiled.

*Sally Brampton from the* Guardian

## Group discussion

As Sally Brampton takes us through her memory of 'The Golden Time' she constructs the writing around a series of word-pictures, each made vivid by the inclusion of important details. It is as if we are being shown Sally Brampton's private photograph album.

If we imagine each of these word-pictures as a photograph and give each one a title we can examine it closely, seeing how the detail is built up. For instance, the first picture could be entitled 'Grandfather Alone'. It might include the following details: waistcoat, blue eyes, books with biro titles, sugar, etc.

Finish adding the other details to 'Grandfather Alone' yourselves and then discuss each of these other pictures and write down all the details that would be included in it:

| | |
|---|---|
| Grandfather and Grandmother | The Park |
| The City | The Man |
| Sally in the Garden | September |
| Together in the Restaurant | |

You may feel that there are more pictures in the passage; if so, title and describe them in the same way.

## Suggestion for writing

'The Golden Time' is the recollection of a special time, and the people and places associated with it. You may have a memory like this which you feel will always be with you, triggered by thoughts of a particular place or people that you particularly loved. It might, for instance, be a summer holiday or a friendship.

Write about your own 'Golden Time'. Try using Sally Brampton's technique of adding in small details – take your readers through your own photo album of that 'Golden Time'. You may, in fact, have some real photographs of the time that you could use to help you write.

# Extensions

The books used in this unit are:

*Dressing For Breakfast* by Stephanie Calman (Fontana, 1988)
*My Left Foot* by Christy Brown (Secker and Warburg, 1954)
'The Golden Time' is an article from the *Guardian*

The subject of first love has been written about over and over again. If it is a subject that interests you then you could read some other books that deal with this theme. For instance:

**Plays**
*Romeo and Juliet* by Shakespeare
*A View from the Bridge* by Arthur Miller
*P'Tang Yang Kipperbang* by Jack Rosenthal
*Gregory's Girl* by Bill Forsyth

**Poems**
'Meeting 1944' by George Szirtes
'Nessa' by Paul Durcan

**Short stories**
'Mort' by John Wain
'Flight' by Doris Lessing
'The Osage Orange Tree' by William Stafford

**Novels**
*The Basketball Game* by Julius Lester
*Wuthering Heights* by Emily Brontë
*The Beautiful Visit* by Elizabeth Jane Howard
*Fair Stood the Wind for France* by H. E. Bates
*Invitation to the Waltz* by Rosamond Lehmann
*Flambards* by K. M. Peyton
*A Room With a View* by E. M. Forster
*Sons and Lovers* by D. H. Lawrence
*Women in Love* by D. H. Lawrence

# 3 FAR FROM HOME

This unit deals with the joys and terrors of being in a strange place. The extracts range from Martha Gellhorn's experience of racial prejudice in Haiti to Joe Simpson's brush with death on a mountain peak in the Andes.

The unit begins, however, much closer to home, with a fascinating chance to see Britain through the eyes of the African writer Buchi Emecheta as she tries to come to terms with living in the place she calls 'Pussy Cat Mansions'.

# PUSSY CAT MANSIONS

In her book, *In the Ditch*, Buchi Emecheta tells the story of her arrival in Britain and her struggle to set herself up as a writer. In her foreword to the book she explains why she chose to write in the third person, referring to herself as Adah. Adah, she says, represents her earlier self – a different person from the successful author of today. She describes Adah's background like this:

Adah, who is an Ibo from Nigeria, arrived in London in 1962 to join her husband, to whom she was married in 1959, and bring her babies. She and her husband thought it would be wise to bring up their children in England, while they, the parents, read for higher degrees. They would then go back to Nigeria, loaded with academic and maybe athletic honours. But their plans miscarried from the beginning. Adah did not bargain for the social structure she was to find in England; she expected to have to live frugally and in simple quarters, but she had no idea how difficult it would be to find accommodation of any kind, nor did she dream that she would have to live in conditions which would have been intolerable at home. Her husband became, in her eyes at least, a changed man; the marriage crumbled and separation, which would have been inconceivable with five babies at home in Nigeria, was the logical step in England.

Adah is understandably delighted when she is offered a council flat and she moves into 'Pussy Cat Mansions' with high hopes.

The Pussy Cat Mansions were built round a large compound. Adah called the open space a compound, remembering Africa. The Family Adviser, whom she met later, used the word courtyard for the open space. It was an open space into which all the front doors opened out. In the centre of the compound were some ill-looking buildings. Adah's African friends called these little houses 'Juju man's house'. When the vicar's wife visited, she said to Adah, 'Those houses look like a monastery,' but the deaconess said they looked more like a mortuary. Originally the architect had meant them to be used as pram and bicycle sheds, but by the time Adah moved into the Mansions the sheds had deteriorated so much that few mums would dream of putting their prams in them.

The Mansions kids decided to make better use of these ill-looking buildings. They would rescue any piece of old furniture, any piece of old clothing, or any type of article which they fancied from the rubbish dumps, and deposit them in the little houses. The little houses ended up by looking more like a hippy shrine than anything else.

There were nearly one hundred and forty flats in the Mansions. The ground-floor flats were mainly one-room flats for the very old and infirm. The arrangement was perfect as most of the old people at the Mansions had meals brought to them 'on wheels', and the people who brought the meals were saved from climbing those endless stairs. The only disadvantage was the Mansion kids. The open space was used by the kids as a playground and on summer evenings the playground looked like a circus. Big boys and girls cycled round the little houses, dogs barking and yelping at their heels; some boys played organized games of football, while a lot more would engage in just throwing balls, broken milk bottles and stones at random. Of course the old folk on the ground floor were usually the victims of the noise, the stone throwing and the dogs' noise. There was little they could do about it so they just accepted things as they were.

Probably the old folk were consoling themselves for the fact that, after all, they did not have long to live. To save them from unnecessary accidents, most of their windows had barbed wire fixed on them, just like prison windows where murderers waited for execution. The barbed wire was meant to protect the windows from the boys' balls smashing them, but the picture they gave was that of condemnation, unwantedness and death – so impersonal and unclean did they look.

The stairs leading to the top flats were of grey stone, so steep were they that it took Adah and her kids weeks to get used to them. They were always smelly with a thick lavatorial stink. Most of the rubbish chutes along the steps and balconies were always overflowing and always open, their contents adding to the stink. The walls along the steep steps were of those old shiny, impersonal bricks still seen in old tube stations, but even more like those Adah had seen in films of prisons. The windows were small and so were the doors. Most of the flats were dark in sympathy with the dark atmosphere. Ah, yes, the Mansions were a unique place, a separate place individualized for 'problem families'. Problem families with real problems were placed in a problem place. So even if one lived at the Mansions and had no problems the set-up would create problems – in plenty.

Adah's problems were many. How to study, keep her job and look after her kids. Looking after her kids was one of the problems created for her by the Mansions set-up. In her old place her fear was that the landlord might harm them. At the Mansions, it was a different fear: offending the neighbours.

The walls separating one flat from the other were so thin that you could hear your next-door neighbour cough. In such a set-up how could a single girl keep four active children and a yelling baby from disturbing the neighbours?

Three days after she moved into the Mansions a man, a very angry man but very small indeed, knocked at her door. She was so surprised at the loudness of the knock that she went to the door with a frown on her face. She staggered backwards at the small man's voice. His voice was so big that she was tempted to look behind him for another owner of the voice. It was so incredible, such a loud voice from such a small man. Somebody said somewhere that Mother Nature is always logical. Well, with this Mr Small, she had miscalculated.

'Look!' he thundered, not bothering to introduce himself or excuse himself. 'Look, I don't mind your colour!' Adah jumped. Colour, what colour was he talking about; she had never seen Mr Small before: what colour was he referring to? Well, human nature being what it is, Adah looked at the colour of the back of her hand, well yes. Mr Small did not mind the colour brown, now what next? What is the next thing he did not mind about? Mr Small's eyes followed her movements and smiled. Happy. He had put Adah in her place. A black person must always have a place, a white person already had one by birthright.

'My baby is only three weeks old. You and your kids kept him awake all night, what did you think you were doing, eh? And you walking about with them army boots. I won't have it, I am warning yer.'

Adah was puzzled. She tried to work out the argument in her mind. But two points did not quite fit in. One was her colour, which Mr Small did not mind, and secondly the army boots. So she asked, 'Are you sure you heard army boots in the night? You see, there is no man here and I don't wear army boots, because, you see, I've never been in the army.'

Mr Small went hysterical and his equally little wife joined him. It seemed that since Adah and her kids moved into the Mansions the Small family had never had a moment's peace. This brought out Mr Small's mother, a little woman with white hair and white whiskers. Adah knew that to argue was going to be a losing battle. She was made to understand by Granny Small that Mr Small was born in the Mansions, and that Mrs Small was also born in the Mansions, just from the flat opposite. Adah got the message, she was dealing with The Establishment, one of the original clans of the Mansions who had lived there for thirty years. She was being told to mind her ways, because the Council would rather listen to reports from the Mansions' senior citizens than to the story of a newcomer. It was going to be a case of her story against theirs.

'I am sorry about the disturbance. I'll tell the kids to make less noise.' That was her first mistake. At the Mansions, it was not normal to apologize. Even when you were caught stealing, you had to argue your way out. If arguments failed, you could always fight your way out of any mess. To say you were sorry was like signing your death warrant. It was a sign of weakness. You were inviting the other person to overcome you, suppress you.

The Smalls seemed happy to show Adah their new baby. So Adah's old man had deserted her? They tut-tutted their sympathy. Of course she could always ask them for any help. They were always willing to help.

The Smalls were just one of the few families in the Manions who started poor and ended up rich – rich by Mansions standards, at any rate. There was the Granny Small who came into the Mansions as a widow thirty years ago with six kids. Most of them had married and gone, leaving Mr Small and his pretty wife. Mr Small worked as a plumber for the Council, and tradition had it that he was very hard-working and that the family were consequently very rich. They got everything from the Mothercare shop, and they would like the dregs, the usual unmarried mothers, or the wife of 'Bill who was sent down the other day', to know that they were in a class higher.

Adah knew that to quarrel with their type would be useless, so she decided to be friends. But how does one become friends with someone who believes that he is superior, richer and made of a better clay? Still, she was determined to try.

One of the methods she had found very helpful in securing friendship in England was to pretend to be stupid. You see, if you were black and stupid, you were conforming to what society expected of you. She was determined to try it with the Smalls.

Her opportunity came the day after. It had been very wet, and she was beginning to realize how damp it could be in the Mansions flats. Some men were delivering coalite, and seeing the Smalls buying some, she thought she might buy some too. She thought coalite would be easy to light. She tried and tried again, but the coalite did not start. She knew she could pour paraffin on it and start it quickly, but was not quite sure that it would not start a fire.

With her eyes streaming from smoke, and her hands blackened by the coalite, she came out of the balcony and luckily Granny Small was standing there.

'Please, how do I light the coalite? I don't seem to be getting it right.' Granny Small turned and faced her. Her eyes were bloodshot. Adah regretted her impulsive gesture immediately. She should have stayed indoors, she should have kept trying until she got it right. She could not go back now without appearing eccentric. So she repeated her plea, now in a voice unnecessarily loud.

'I can't light my coalite.'

'Well, why did you buy it? What am I supposed to do about it, eh?'

The pretty wife shot out. 'What was it, Mum?'

'She couldn't light the coalite.' Well, what were they going to hear next?

Adah pointed out that she knew she could start it with paraffin, but would it start a fire? The pretty wife screamed. 'Mum, she's going to bring in the firemen soon. Oh my God, what are we in for!' Her shrieking voice brought out more neighbours, some to see what the matter was, but most to have a good look at the new tenant as if she was a wonder from outer space.

This method had never failed her before. Why did it fail with the Smalls? They did not even give her time to get to know her before they passed their judgement. Being friendly with them would be out of the question. She would have to mind her own business. What these people felt towards her was resentment. She had worsened the situation by making them know that she had never used coalite before. How could she have known how to use coalite? She was born and brought up in the tropics where the average daily temperature was always in the eighties. How could people be so ignorant? The funniest thing was that from the cynical remarks made around her, they implied that she must have been illiterate not to know how to use coalite.

What was the point in explaining to them that in her country she attended a colonial school with a standard equalling the best girls' schools in London? What was the point in telling them that she was not illiterate as they thought, and that even here in their country she worked in their Civil Service? She looked at them, felt a little bit like being sick, then walked in, shutting her front door with a loud bang.

Inside she poured paraffin on some paper, and started the fire. She did not have to call in the firemen, because there was no need for them. She did not burn the flats down.

Adah knew that her problems were going to be many, for the Smalls seemed determined to add to the fact that she would have to worry about keeping her job, worry about how to study, and now worry how to keep the kids quiet. If the Mansions tenants did not want her, well, she was going to be different.

She was not going to be like the other separated mums. At the Manions, mums with kids and no husbands did not go out to work. It was just not done. If you were a separated mum, you lived on the dole. 'I am going to be different,' Adah said to herself in consolation, little realizing that she was human, a lonely woman, who more than anybody else would need people to talk to and be friendly with.

She not only had to conform, but for peace's sake, she had to belong. She had to belong, socialize, participate in the goings-on.

*from* In the Ditch *by Buchi Emecheta*

## Group discussion

- Discuss the following statements about the extract and decide which you agree with and which you do not. You must have evidence to back up your decisions.

   (a) Pussy Cat Mansions is ideal for old people.

   (b) Mr Small came down to Adah to complain because her children had kept his baby awake.

   (c) Mr Small is not racist.

   (d) The Smalls are eager to help Adah.

   (e) Adah does not handle Mr Small well.

   (f) Adah is depressed by her experience.

- During this extract, the Smalls never treat Adah in a blatantly racist manner and yet there is a constant undercurrent of racism. As the writer says, 'A black person must always have a place, a white person already has one by birthright.' Examine the way that the Smalls behave towards Adah and the way in which she responds. How does Buchi Emecheta give the impression of underlying racism?

## Suggestions for writing

I  Pussy Cat Mansions seems to be a place that is full of stories. Adah's is one of them, but Buchi Emecheta hints that there are many more young women struggling to bring up children alone in the Mansions. We also hear briefly of 'Bill who was sent down the other day'. Write another story from Pussy Cat Mansions. You could include Adah and the Smalls in your story or make use of Bill and his wife.

**2** Many people have experienced the problems that Adah faces when she tries to fit into the British way of life. Perhaps your parents came from another country to settle in Britain, or you may have moved here when you were a young child. If so, write about your experiences and those of your parents. You may need to do some research by interviewing your family about their early experiences in Britain.

OR

Write a story that deals with the experiences of someone newly arrived in Britain. You could write it in the form of the memories of a fictional character, thinking back to his or her early days in this country.

# WHITE INTO BLACK

Buchi Emecheta experienced thinly-veiled racism when she arrived in Britain, but in Haiti Martha Gellhorn encounters blatant abuse. She finds this all the more shocking because, as a white middle-aged woman, she is unused to it.

Before you read on, it might be useful to know a little about the history of Haiti. During the eighteenth and early nineteenth centuries it was a French colony called Saint Domengue, notorious for its brutality to slaves. Martha Gellhorn describes the island at that time as a 'forerunner of Nazi concentration camps'. Eventually, through the struggle of the great slave-leader, Toussaint L'Ouverture, Haiti gained independence and became, with Liberia, the first modern free state governed by blacks. Its political history has always been stormy, and soon after Martha Gellhorn's visit in 1957, 'Papa Doc' Duvalier took power. He was a dictator who kept his power by terrorising the people with a secret police force known as the Tonton Macoutes who used voodoo magic to instil fear. When Duvalier died, his son, 'Baby Doc', succeeded him, ruling in much the same way.

Martha Gellhorn chose to go to Haiti on a whim, hoping to find somewhere quiet in which to write a novel. However, from the moment of her arrival, one disaster follows another.

Arriving in Port-au-Prince, she decides to leave for Jacmel, an isolated town that she thinks will be more peaceful than the capital. While she is waiting for transport she is invited to a Voodoo ceremony which turns

out to be depressing and frightening. On her way back to her hotel, she slips and twists her ankle.

She arrives limping in Jacmel to find that the only hotel is the Pension Croft where she receives an icy welcome from Madame Croft and is given an extremely uncomfortable room. At dinner that evening everyone stares at her and giggles. She soon realises that she is the only white person in Jacmel and that the inhabitants are racist.

In desperation she goes exploring in Jacmel and is delighted at last to find the public library and the librarian, Monsieur Réné.

[. . .] I asked Monsieur Réné if there was any other foreigner here. Such as a foreigner washed ashore from a wreck with permanent brain damage, or a criminal foreigner hiding from the cops of three countries. Monsieur Réné was puzzled by my question. No, he said, we are all Haitians. Foreigners never come here; our village offers no distractions. I saw it, then. I was the only Negro in Jacmel. And, furthermore, a Negro who had gate-crashed an exclusive white club, the Pension Croft. The Pension Croft, I lied, was very nice but a bit noisy; could I rent a quieter room in someone's house? Monsieur Réné was amazed. The houses were filled with large families, nobody would wish to take in a guest. Not surprising. Few white families would welcome an unknown black visitor. I dared not ask, so soon, about transport back to Port-au-Prince, but when I did Monsieur Réné had no ideas; he never went himself; his car was not strong enough and Port-au-Prince seemed too far, too strange; no one from Jacmel went there.

Beyond the main library with its two rows of bookshelves, Monsieur Réné ushered me into an oversized empty closet. They found a table and chair, the window was luxury, the silence blessed. Since I hadn't brought anything with me, might I just sit here? Monsieur Réné hurried to find a writing-pad and two pencils and left on tiptoe so that creation could begin. I wrote on the pad 'Self pity, that way madness lies,' then stretched out on the clean floor, to rest my ankle. Monsieur Réné knocked and entered before I could scramble up. In this position, he saw what ailed me, was full of sympathy and insisted on driving me to the clinic.

The clinic has vanished from memory but I remember the smiling doctor, a slightly larger edition of Monsieur Réné, in a white coat. He produced an enormous syringe, suitable for a horse, and a gigantic thick needle, about six inches long. I was paralyzed by my new role, lonely Negro scared to offend white authority. With terror, I let that kind dangerous doctor plunge the needle into my hot puffed ankle and force in what seemed a pint of liquid. Novocaine, said the doctor, all goes well now. Monsieur Réné drove me back to the Pension Croft.

By four that afternoon, my left foot and ankle resembled elephantiasis and the pain was torture. I clamped the pillow over my face and groaned aloud; through the pillow I heard myself making animal noises. I wept torrents. I couldn't stop and was frightened to be so helpless among enemies: shivering, sweating, snivelling, half crazy. Madame Croft told a maid to inquire why the white-Negro was being a nuisance. Madame Croft appeared in the doorway to check for herself. She stared at me with glacial contempt, but did send up pitcher after pitcher of boiling water. For the next three hours I soaked my elephantine extremity in the washbowl and was finally beyond the howling stage. Madame Croft sent up greasy soup. I slept despite the cot smell and gruelling sounds from other rooms.

Suffering is supposed to ennoble; not me, it stupefies me. I could have saved myself by ordering a bottle of rum and getting sodden drunk, and then another bottle, though first finding a telephone to call the US Consulate in Port-au-Prince and demand evacuation on medical grounds. I thought drink was for pleasure among friends and never turned to consulates in an hour of need. In growing misery, I clung to one plan: survive until I could walk, then dump my suitcase and proceed on foot, hippety-hop over the mountains, to an airplane and flight from this doom island.

When I could return to the library, I did not report that the nice doctor had just about finished me but Monsieur Réné saw that I was barely mobile and brought me a cane. My creeping along with a cane, sneaker on right foot, cut-open bedroom slipper on left foot, added to my repellent skin colour, made me an irresistible target. When classes ended at noon the homing schoolchildren picked up stones and cheerfully stoned me. They were behind me and I didn't know what the yelling and laughing was about until a stone hit me. I thought this an accident and turned to smile forgiveness, only to see a bunch of pretty little kids, dressed in those French-style black school smocks, jumping up and down and aiming more stones. Which hit me. 'Blanc! Blanc!' they shouted, meaning 'Nigger! Nigger!' The stones weren't large, nor were the kids; I wasn't hurt. I was an old lame Negro, chivvied and harassed by white kids, and I burned with outrage. And with hatred for those adults on the street who watched, smiling approval.

There was nothing to do except retreat to the library, where again I suppressed the news of the day. The silent retreat shamed me. Shame was hardest to bear. I could see it would take a while to get used to humiliation. If anyone ever got used to it?

My unborn novel was by now a sad joke. All day, I sat on the hard library chair, resting my foot on an orange crate, and read and brooded. From whenever ideas first reach a child's mind, I had been indoctrinated by my parents' words and deeds never to condemn by race, creed, colour or even nationality. The history of our time gave that early teaching the force of moral law; I refer, above all, to the Nazis. But there was still plenty of repression in the world, by race, creed and colour, and I was wholeheartedly against it. Yet here, I sat, in racist Jacmel, grinding my teeth in a fury of counter-racism. I wondered whether I was ruined for life and would become a disgrace to my parents, loathing blacks.

[. . .]

While I was brooding on my chair one morning, Monsieur Réné appeared with a book. He said it was the only book in English in the library, where I was always the only customer. No one could read English but perhaps it would interest me. The book was E. M. Forster's *Two Cheers for Democracy*. A miracle of the highest order. Oh, that beautiful book! It shines with reason, mercy, honour, good will and wit; and is written in those water-smooth sentences that one wants to stroke for the pleasure of feeling them. No longer isolated, I had Mr Forster's mind for company. When I finished the book, I wrote pages to Mr Forster, like a letter in a bottle, telling him that he was a light in the darkness and a moral example to mankind. I resolved to reform. I would not disgrace my parents or Mr Forster; no goddamned black racists were going to make a racist of me.

During these month-long days, I observed the weather but took no joy from it, though it was joyful. The sky went up in pale to darker translucent layers of blue, the air smelled of flowers and sea and sun, so delicious you could taste it. The Caribbean, my favourite sea, stretched out like a great smooth sapphire carpet with wind moving gently under it. I hungered for the sea and one afternoon nerved myself to chance the path down the cliff. With a dress over my bathing-suit, a towel around my neck, the usual footwear and cane, I made my way slowly to the beach. The sand was golden, empty and lovely; no boats, no people and no sign of there having been either.

I chucked my stuff and got into the sea like a crab, using my arms. Freedom returned; I could move. I swam far out in the silky water and floated, rejoicing. Jacmel washed off me, body and soul. Unable to sing, a felt lack, I made shouting noises of delight. Every day, until I had two sound legs, I would bring bread and papaya, the only edible pension food, to this glorious beach and swim and sunbathe. Happiness was possible, even in Jacmel.

When I started to drag myself up the sand to my clothes, I saw the boys. They were playing ball with my dress, footwear, cane, towel. There were eight of them, teenagers, fleet of foot and laughing their heads off. I stood up, with dignity, and informed them that they were too big for this game and please give me my effects. They instantly invented a new game. They ran in close and flicked me with dress and towel, twirled my sneaker against my face, feinted and jabbed with the cane. After lurching once for my dress, I realized that pleased them; also that it was useless. I imagined, with dread, hobbling up the street in my white bathing-suit while all Jacmel came out to jeer. But I could not make it, not without foot covering and cane.

I limped on the comfortable sand towards the path, maintaining cold silence and, I hoped, a calm face. They followed, same game, same taunting laughter. My good resolves left me. I wanted to cause them grievous bodily harm. Failing that, I wanted to curse them at the top of my lungs. But I was afraid to anger these white bully boys. They could do much worse to a defenceless Negro. And who would punish them, who would care? Monsieur René, the tolerant educated white, could hardly stand up to the whole nigger-baiting town. I had to conceal rage and alarm, as other Negroes have surely done, and stand and take it. Suddenly, they had had all the fun they needed, threw my things around the beach, and ran up the path. I collected them piece by piece, got organized, and climbed to the street, knowing I would not risk the sea again. Jacmel had defeated me.

[. . .]

Much later I began to think, imagine, hope, that maybe, somehow, possibly I understood just the tiniest bit of what it really means to be black in a bad place.

*Martha Gellhorn*

## Group discussion

Having read the potted history of Haiti on page 00, discuss the following questions:

- Do you think that there is any historical justification for the way Martha Gellhorn is treated during her stay?

- Is there any hint in this article of the dictatorship which was to come a few years later?

## *Suggestions for writing*

1 For a short while Martha Gellhorn knows something of what it feels like to be black, as she says, 'in a bad place'. Her experience in Haiti has much in common with the stories and films that have been written around the idea of people changing places. You may have seen the film *Trading Places* in which a rich and poor man swap places, or *Big* in which a young boy magically takes on the appearance of a man. There is also a novel by Mary Rodgers called *Freaky Friday* which uses a similar idea but with a mother and daughter, and a rather nasty short story by Ray Bradbury called 'The Playground' in which a father has to suffer the tortures of the local playground in place of his son. These have their roots in an old story by F. Anstey called *Vice Versa* in which a father is forced to go to school instead of his son. Explore this 'changing places' idea in a story of your own.

By some magic or scientific accident a character of your choice is turned into someone else; someone of the kind he or she oppresses either consciously or by accident. Here are some ideas:

(a)   A teacher is turned into a pupil who has problems at school.
(b)   A bully is turned into one of his victims.
(c)   A rich person becomes unemployed and homeless.

Alternatively, you could take your character to an invented country or an alien planet where the social positions are reversed. A man arrives on a planet where women are in control and men are treated as second-class citizens, for instance. How is he treated? What effect does his arrival have on the inhabitants?

2 Write about your own experience of travel, either within the UK or abroad. Have you learned anything from your travels? You could write generally about travelling or concentrate on a particular experience which you feel taught you something.

# *Experiences of prison*

Rosie Johnston was sentenced to nine months in prison in 1986 for dealing in drugs. This young woman from a privileged background suddenly found herself snatched from the comfortable life of Oxford and thrown into a Holloway prison cell. In her book, *Inside Out*, she tells the story of how she coped with the degradation and loneliness. In this episode from the beginning of the book, she gets her first taste of prison life.

## Group discussion

Before you read the extract, discuss in your group what ideas you associate with the word 'prison'. Use a large piece of paper and 'brainstorm' your thoughts until you have filled the sheet with everything you know and feel about prison. It may help if you do the same thing with the word 'home' on another sheet of paper. You will be able to see how the associations of the two words contrast.

# HOLLOWAY

After seeing my parents and my sisters go, I cried for a long time. Mum had given the authorities an unopened packet of cigarettes which was passed on to me. Trying to concentrate on smoking without making a mess of it was a way of occupying myself. I burnt my fingers and dropped a cigarette into my cup of tea. Anything was better than thinking about Mum and Dad driving home, exhausted and miserable, wondering what was happening to me.

Near by, a cell door slammed and someone started to cry. It was a woman sounding desperate. As I sat wondering what she had been punished for, my cell door opened and an officer told me to move. I followed her to a smaller, grimier cell, where I found the person whom I had heard crying.

'You might as well be together,' said the officer. 'You're both going to the same place.'

Prison, of course. But which one? I assumed it would be Holloway, but no one had told me for certain. The officer left, locking us in. I stood by the door saying nothing. My cellmate was sitting on the bench in the corner, slumped against the wall. She did not look like anyone I would have expected to see waiting for transport to prison. She was elegantly dressed, with beautiful shiny black hair and a model's figure. I sat beside her on the bench and offered her a cigarette; she had some of her own. We both lit one and sat blowing smoke into the stuffy air. I told her my name, and asked hers. It was Sarah Ray.

'I know about you,' she said. 'My lawyer told me that I would get the same sentence as you, and that's what happened.'

I also knew her name; hers was also a drug-related offence and my solicitor had said that I would get whatever she was given.

Sarah told me that she had been in court two days earlier and had been sent to Holloway for two days to await sentencing. She had thought that the judge was just trying to frighten her, and that she would get a suspended sentence. She was desperate at the thought of going back, and I was terrified of what lay ahead. Sarah had spent her two days in Holloway in a single cell. She did not talk to anyone, so she had little idea of what to expect from a six-month stretch. I wanted to know details like whether we would be allowed razors with which to shave our armpits. We sat on the bench smoking, wondering what would happen when we had no more cigarettes left. Would we need money? How did inmates pay for cigarettes? I wished I had taken the time to find out about these things. When would we be able to see our families? Did we have to wear a uniform? Sarah said that she hadn't seen anyone wearing one, apart from the 'screws' (two days had been enough to realise that officers were not called officers inside). No one had approached her or tried to rough her up, but then she had been on a wing for unsentenced prisoners, not in the mainstream of the prison.

We made a pact to stick together if we could. She was beautiful, and, as I had guessed, had been a model. She was my age, and we came from a similar background. Because of her reticence and physical appearance, she appeared to be aloof, although after spending hours with her in a cramped cell, I realised that she was just rather shy. If I had met her under normal circumstances, at a party for instance, I would never have thought that we could be friends. Yet in a cell, waiting for transport to hell, I decided that I liked her very much. The value of having someone to talk to, or just to be with, was priceless.

The waiting was making us fraught; we did not know when we would be leaving or where we were going, and no one would answer our questions.

'F— this,' said Sarah, 'I'm going to sing.' She started and I joined in. We lay feet to feet on the narrow bench and sang everything we knew. A screw looked in through the hatch in the cell door. She went away muttering to herself. Sarah and I started to laugh in a hysterical way that might equally have been crying; singing had also been a sort of release for us, a way of relieving the tension.

'How about "New Orleans" to finish off with?' Sarah suggested. As I sang the tears started again.

It was 8 pm when the van arrived; we had been waiting since lunchtime. We were escorted to the court car park and bundled into the back of the van. It was cold, and the streets were inky black. We were both freezing: our thin, court-appearance clothes did nothing to protect us from the cold. Our journey was protracted, for we had to go via Reading to pick up two other convicts, Jean and Rita, who had been given four and seven years respectively for smuggling heroin. When they found out the length of our sentences, it was clear that they thought Sarah and I were small fry. They had both been on remand, and so did not have to cope with the terror of uncertainty. They laughed and joked their way to London as if they were on a day-trip to Bangor, while Sarah and I huddled in the back, hardly saying a word. The van rattled along, a grille separating the driver from his unwholesome passengers. I wondered if I would be able to keep a diary. Would they provide writing material for 'cons'?

As we drove down Parkhurst Road, we were given a perfunctory 'Nearly there, girls' by one of the escort screws. I found the word 'girls' humiliating. It reminded me of a school outing, which was the last thing we were on.

It was dark, so I couldn't see much as the van swung left and stopped outside grey gates. A blue plaque, with the words HMP Holloway, shone in the orange light. The sickly neon guided the van through the security procedure. The first gate opened and shut behind us. We were caught in a vacuum, a prisoners' purgatory, while the guard checked us. The second gate opened and we were in the prison itself. I was hit by a wave of physical terror. My stomach contracted and I gripped Sarah, who looked green in the deceiving light. It was as if a giant hand was pressing a cork into a jar in which I was to be sealed, like a specimen in a laboratory. Shakily, we climbed out of the van and were ordered to wait in Reception. There we were finger-printed, strip-searched and photographed for our 'mug shots'. I did what I was told and followed instructions like a zombie, my eyes blinking beneath Home Office lights.

During the strip-search, I remembered that I wasn't wearing any knickers. The screw in charge was shocked. 'A nice girl like you?' she queried as she issued me with two pairs of cherry-motif prison department pants. Apart from what I was issued with, I had nothing but the clothes I stood up in.

At the next desk I was given my prison number, D29510. I was then sent into a dingy room to await further instructions. I sat with Jean and Rita, who were talking about the 'bloody kangas'. They seemed friendly enough and I asked them what it meant.

'Rhyming slang, love. Kangaroo, screw.' At which they burst out laughing. Jean and Rita knew the ropes. They talked a little about their case, claiming that it had been a set-up. They were really prostitutes, they said.

We were given a plate of doughnuts. I bit into mine and then put it down. 'There's no jam in the middle,' I said, without thinking.

One of the screws overheard and pounced on the chance I had given her. 'Look dear, we are in prison now, not Buckingham Palace.' Jean and Rita thought it hilarious. I sat miserably, failing to join in the joke.

We were all issued with a bag of toiletries, a towel and a pair of floral pyjamas. Sarah and I had been trailing from desk to desk, screw to screw, without speaking. Just as I turned to say something to her, she was taken away. She was going to a different wing to the one I was to be on. We had forgotten about the likelihood of separation. We did not know if we would see each other again.

*from* Inside Out *by Rosie Johnston*

## Group discussion (cont.)

- Go back to your 'Prison Brainstorm' sheet. Was Rosie Johnston's experience as you expected? Did she feel the way that you thought she would?

- When she reaches Holloway, Rosie says, 'I was hit by a wave of physical terror.' Why is she so terrified of what is to come? In your group discuss what it is about prison that we all find frightening.

- How do Rosie and Sarah cope with their terror? Look through the passage again and discuss how their fears make them speak and act.

- What is your opinion of the way that the prisoners are treated during this time?

Now compare Rosie Johnston's experiences of prison life with Daniel De Souza's account below of the way a Turkish prison deals with young offenders.

# TURAN

In 1975 Daniel De Souza was arrested attempting to smuggle cannabis into Turkey. He was sentenced to imprisonment for life but was eventually released after serving twelve years. He soon became hardened by the cruelty of prison life. However, in this extract from his book, *Under a Crescent Moon*, he tells the story of how he was touched by the plight of a new prisoner, Turan, who was only eight years old.

'Geh vedi, geh vedi, cos here I com.'

There was something odd about the thin, wailing voice singing the refrain repeatedly. It took me several minutes, hovering between sleep and wakefulness, to solve the puzzle. The words were barely English, the melody distorted, yet I recognized it as the chorus line from the American hit song 'Get Ready'. Once it had been a favourite and hearing it again after so many years, I felt a rush of nostalgia.

But who could be singing such a song on a winter's morning in a Turkish prison? Reluctantly, I left my warm nest beneath a pile of blankets and ventured out of my cell into the icy, draughty corridor.

The sound came from outside the block, yet when I first peered down into the courtyard, it looked empty. Then I saw a tiny figure huddled in the only corner touched by the watery dawn sunshine. A shorn head poked out from a shapeiess, outsized jacket. The child was a new arrival at the juvenile block facing the foreigners' wing. He was trying to shield his bare feet from the cold by drawing them up inside his thin prison-issue trousers.

Returning to my cell, I rummaged through boxes of belongings for old socks, a sweater and a pair of plastic shower sandals. I took them down the stairs to the courtyard gate and called through the bars to the boy.

He could hardly control his shivering hands long enough to put on the socks. When he stripped off his jacket to don the sweater, I glimpsed his emaciated chest. His ribs protruded so starkly that he looked deformed. His fingers were covered in chilblains. At a guess, he was no more than eight years old with features showing him to be an *arap*, mixed blood. The whites of his eyes contrasted strongly with his dark complexion.

Having put on all the clothes, he flashed such a wide grin, I had to ask, 'Are you hungry?'

I only had milk and biscuits to offer but he wolfed them down. In a spray of crumbs, he told me his name was Turan and his crime was the theft of two oranges. Incredulous, I asked, 'Two oranges?'

'Well, I've only got two hands. I couldn't carry more,' he replied flatly.

He told me that he was eleven years old and showed me his prison identity card. Then, having looked round cautiously to see if anybody was watching, he took out an old plastic wallet from his trouser pocket and extracted his most prized possession, a Polaroid photograph of a hefty black GI cradling a baby.

'He's my Dad, holding me when I was little,' he said, proudly.

That explained the American pop song. 'Did he teach you English?' I asked.

Turan scowled and mumbled softly, 'Not much. I was only six when he left.' Then, more cheerful, 'When I'm bigger he's going to come back and take me home. To the United States of America.'

He hesitated over 'home'. He sounded awed by the United States of America. This was his dream for the future.

He hardly mentioned his mother. From different remarks pieced together, I understood she had deserted him when he was still very young. Since then, he had been living in an uncle's garage where he worked as an apprentice mechanic.

'Don't you go to school?' I asked. 'School!' he answered scornfully. 'I've never been near one. I'll learn to read and write when I get to America.'

His story was familiar. Although attendance at primary school was compulsory, the law was rarely enforced. Parents on starvation wages couldn't afford school uniforms, books and pencils. Similarly, there were laws forbidding child labour but the pittance earned by children helped families survive.

Matter-of-factly, Turan described how his uncle, unable to afford the expense of keeping an extra child, had taken him to the Izmir State Orphanage. Turan had spent several hours exploring the spacious grounds, romping with other orphans, before being interviewed by the administrators.

His delight in recalling what must have been an intensely enjoyable experience suddenly vanished. Shaking his head with baffled despair, he choked, 'They wouldn't take me. I don't know why.' After a long silence, on the verge of tears, he turned aside to hide his face.

I also had to turn away – to hide my anger. I thought my years behind bars had toughened me but the kid's story of being excluded even from an orphanage was too cruel.

By then, some of the other children had emerged from the block and were crouching in the sunlit corner of the courtyard. Turan eyed them apprehensively.

The kid deserved a break. I saw Orhan stumbling sleepily into the yard and called out to him.

Orhan, barely sixteen, had already served four years in the juvenile block for armed robbery. Extremely tough and vicious, he was feared even by the guards. The administration had made him chief of the juveniles, hoping that the responsibility would blunt his rebellion.

Orhan swaggered over. The hand on his hip gripped a knife concealed under his shirt. Turan took one look at him and sidled fearfully away.

I offered Orhan a cigarette. He planted it in the corner of his mouth where it accentuated his ugly sneer. Despite the bitter cold, he wore only a t-shirt and pyjamas. With his bare arms crossed to display crude pictures of a knife and pistol, tattooed in the prison with inked razor blades, he slouched against the bars.

We began with the usual small talk. Then I pointed to Turan. 'He was delivered this morning. I want you to go easy on him.'

Orhan's sneer widened into a cocky grin. 'What's in it for me?'

I gave him the almost full packet of cigarettes. 'That's just a start.'

He slipped the cigarettes into his pocket and drawled, 'It's OK with me, but what about my friends?'

I knew what he meant. The sodomy rites with which juvenile prisoners initiated newcomers to their block were common knowledge throughout the prison. The kids' crude jokes portrayed the ritual as a manhood test. Living opposite the juveniles, the foreigners were often woken in the night by the muffled, agonized screams of kids being raped. They all seemed to recover quickly yet it was important to me that Turan should be spared such torture.

Orhan sensed my concern. He threatened ominously, 'There'll be no problems in the future but I can't guarantee tonight.'

I looked him straight in the eye. 'You can do better than that, Orhan. You're responsible for the block. If Turan passes a peaceful night, there'll be no trouble. If anybody wakes him, you'll regret it.' I reached out to grasp his t-shirt and pulled him violently against the bars. 'Don't forget what happened to Tana.'

The story of Tana, a teenager murdered in Istanbul Prison, was known throughout Turkey. Tana and his gang of knife-toting juveniles had terrorized adult inmates, operating a shakedown racket in the corridors. When it got out of hand, the prisoners hired a professional killer to shoot him. It would have taken only a word to the politicals or a little money in a *Kabadai's** pocket to have Orhan similarly dealt with. I wasn't bluffing and Orhan knew it. There were no screams that night.

The juvenile block was the most deprived and sordid wing in the prison. Aged between eight and seventeen, one hundred and twenty children lived in a block equipped with thirty-eight bunks, two toilets and one tap. They had no chairs, tables or cupboards, only a television.

Loaves of bread and two tanks of watered-down vegetable stew were thrust through the door each day. They became the instant focus of a desperate scramble. Lacking spoons or plates, the younger children pounced wildly on the tanks, scooping up the scorching stew with their fingers. In a frenzy, they stuffed their mouths to bursting point before the fully-grown juveniles kicked them away.

Once a fortnight, the whole block was herded off to the bath-house. With great whoops and whistles, they filed out of the block and down to a domed, tiled basement *hamam*. Issued with bars of primitive soap, they had ten minutes to wash their bodies and uniforms. Without towels or dry clothes, they returned shivering like drenched kittens. The showers weren't much help. The block teemed with lice, rats and cockroaches. Many of the children suffered from skin diseases and they had no money to buy the ointments prescribed by the prison doctor.

Orhan took care of Turan and grew fond of him. Although virtually a slave to the tattoo-scarred block chief and his gang of mini-thugs, Turan was fortunate. He received enough food, ate from a plate with a wooden spoon and had clean bedding.

---

*Bodyguard – imprisoned gangsters were allowed to bring their own bodyguard*

Over the next three months he thrived. He grew at an astonishing rate, filling out, attaining a lean, healthy sleekness until he was scarcely recognizable as the undernourished wretch I first encountered. He proved to be a promising footballer. Scampering barefooted after the rag ball, he learnt to swerve, dribble and pass skilfully.

The kids' spirits never failed to amaze me. Despite their miserable conditions they were always boisterous and enthusiastic, singing, shouting and playing away the days. They had no real contact with jailhouse discipline. Once a week the *hoja*, teacher, visited and lectured them on morality and religion.

The entire block was made to squat silently in the courtyard by truncheon-carrying soldiers while the black-bearded *hoja* talked. Turan became an expert at disrupting the lessons, catapulting paper darts to sting the back of the *hoja*'s neck. Frequently he felt the lash of the *hoja*'s strap but, because of his size, the strokes were less violent than those used on the older boys.

During those first three months Turan's personality also filled out. He became more confident, cheerful and talkative. He lost his fear of prison and began to enjoy the comradeship and unruly life. He also began to ape Orhan's swagger and curses. In the spring of 1981 he was released from prison. Two weeks later he was back on a burglary charge.

Dressed in a flashy new shirt and expensive shoes, bought from the proceeds of burglaries, he was welcomed back by Orhan like a younger brother. He was the same dreamy kid, inventing complex stories of how his father had written to summon him to America and how his uncle, jealous and fearful of losing a worker, had destroyed the letter. Again, he became popular amongst the kids by terrorizing the *hoja*.

However naughty, he remained sweet-natured, with a strong sense of justice and personal honour. When the other children trapped a rat and were dangling it over a fire in the courtyard, Turan stopped the slow torture by killing it outright with a brick. One night he braved the anger of the older juveniles, shouting for the guards to halt the ritual rape of another kid. Whenever Orhan called him, Turan immediately rushed to his side. He became Orhan's knife-keeper, ensuring the weapon was always sharp, clean and instantly available. The children feared Orhan, so Turan, his knife-keeper, was also someone to be approached with caution. As Turan's prestige rose, his devotion to Orhan was more apparent. One day, his hero-worship cropped up in a conversation I had with Prosecutor Shefki Levent.

Shefki Levent was in charge of Shrinigar, one of the three specialized juvenile detention centres in Turkey. An ageing yet dynamic man, he was renowned for his liberal and humanitarian views. Shefki often visited our block to practise his English. All the foreign prisoners looked on him as a friend.

From the window of our block he stood watching Turan playing football in the courtyard. Frowning, he sighed, 'I wish I could take him with me. None of these kids should be here. But there's nothing I can do. Shrinigar is overcrowded. Besides, to be considered he'd have to be sentenced and, without money for a lawyer, we can't bring his case to court.'

One outcome of Shefki's visit was that Orhan and two older boys were switched to an adult block and had no further contact with Turan.

For a time, Turan was calmer. He even started the informal literacy lessons. I convinced him that, with an education, he'd be able to work in a bank where he could steal far more money than any bank robber – enough to fly to America. The idea caught on. A dozen illiterate kids gathered each morning beside the courtyard gate, where I gave them lessons in writing, reading and arithmetic. They all had the same ambition – to leave prison and become bank clerks.

The lessons didn't continue for long. Too many children hung around interrupting the classes. Halef, the teenager appointed by Shefki as the new block chief, didn't have Orhan's sense of leadership. He was too lenient and unconcerned. Turan and some other kids were always challenging his authority. There were constant fights and uproar.

The noise the kids made was overwhelming so I talked with the prosecutor. I tried to persuade him to open the prison school. He let me talk and then answered, 'You don't understand. Officially, there are no children in Turkish prisons so how can I open a school for children who don't exist?'

A week later, minutes before a group of Justice Ministry officials arrived to inspect the foreigners' living conditions, the prosecutor ordered the children's eviction. It made no sense until Head Guard Jasim Baba told me, 'He has to. If the Justice Ministry men look out any window of your block and see the state of the kids, it would cause no end of trouble.'

The juveniles ended up in a disused basement workshop, with no bunks or courtyard for exercise. Two months passed before they returned to the block opposite the foreigners.

Over the next five years, conditions for the juvenile prisoners improved considerably. Teenage inmates were transferred to another block away from the youngsters so there was no more male rape. A school was opened for the adult prisoners but the kids were also made to attend. However, hygiene, health, clothing and food problems were never solved.

My friendship with Turan slowly lost its warmth. He joined the gang of tough kids who skived off from the prison school where I worked. He was in and out of prison half a dozen times for assorted misdemeanours. At the age of fifteen, he moved to the block for teenage inmates and I didn't see him for more than a year.

When I next met him, Turan was a strapping seventeen-year-old. I was walking down the corridor with Head Guard Ismail and Turan rushed straight into us. Ismail went on, leaving me standing alone with Turan. 'That was close,' he winked. 'If he knew what I've got here I'd be in the slammer.' He flashed his uniform jacket open to show me the bottle of codeine cough-mixture fixed under his belt. I saw the outline of a flat knife at the back of his hip.

'Where're you bunking?' I began. 'What's the rap this time?'

'Right now I'm still with the juveniles, but next week they're shifting me to Ibrahim's,' Turan grinned with pride. Sensing my disbelief at his mention of the block reserved for hardened criminals and lifers, he went on, 'This time I'm on a mugging rap. The bitch had to be stitched up so they're throwing the book at me. But I'm still under age.' He shrugged, 'They can't give me much.'

Leaving him, I remembered a sick friend in with the juveniles. 'By the way, Sadik's in your block. You owe me one. Give him a message, will you?'

'What's in it for me?' He gave me a shrewd glance.

I remembered that first morning when Turan had squatted shivering in the courtyard, singing to himself.

'You're right,' I conceded. 'You don't owe me anything.'

*from* Under a Crescent Moon *by Daniel De Souza*

## Group discussion

- Reading Turan's story, we get a glimpse of a world very different from our own; life in a Turkish prison probably seems utterly unlike our idea of what prisons are like.

  Look back over the passage and extract as much information as you can about the way that Turkish prisons are run. Make a list of what you find out.

  Discuss the aspects of prison life that seem to you to be most different from our own prison system. Do these differences make Turkish prison life better or worse?

- Turan progresses from being a hungry orphan who steals two oranges to being a violent mugger. Using the evidence in the passage, discuss who or what is responsible for this decline. Here are three questions to help you focus your discussion.

  (a) Which aspects of the prison, in your view, are accountable for turning Turan into a hardened criminal?

  (b) At the end of the passage De Souza says that Turan does not owe him any favours. Is Turan's subsequent criminal life in fact partially De Souza's fault?

  (c) How might Turan's progression to serious crime have been prevented?

## Suggestions for writing

1 Imagine that as part of an attempt to rehabilitate him, a social worker is brought in to interview Turan. Write a version of this interview in which the social worker tries to establish Turan's past and the reasons behind his criminal life. Start by thinking of some interesting questions for the social worker to ask. You could try this as a piece of drama. Improvise the interview in pairs: one as Turan and the other as the social worker. Finish the assignment by writing the social worker's report on Turan.

2 Write a story which charts a young boy or girl's criminal life in Britain. You could write in the third person or you could tell it

through the eyes of the young person who finds him or herself in a detention centre or prison and is thinking back. Remember, it is important in a story like this to be as realistic as possible and for your central character to be in some way sympathetic, otherwise your readers will not care wht happens to him or her. Use Rosie Johnston's account of her introduction to prison life to help you but to ensure that your story is realistic you could do some research. Here are some ideas to help you.

(a) If sociology is taught in your school, speak to the teacher responsible and ask for the case study of a juvenile criminal. These are usually available in sociology textbooks.

(b) Look in your school or local library for books on juvenile crime. These will help with the details of the law.

(c) Read more extracts from books written by people who have been to prison. There is a list of such books at the end of this unit on page 98.

(d) 'The Loneliness of a Long Distance Runner' by Alan Sillitoe is a short story that deals with the thoughts and experiences of a young offender.

# Travellers' Tales

Travellers have always been adventurers and from the earliest times audiences have been fascinated by travellers' tales. This tradition is far from dead, as Redmond O'Hanlon proves in the next extract taken from his book *Into the Heart of Borneo.*

# THE WELCOME PARTY

O'Hanlon, an ornithologist by profession, specialises in exploring far-flung corners of the world with a friend and the minimum of equipment. On this expedition he chose to take as his companion James Fenton, a poet and journalist. When he asked Fenton to accompany him on his next trip, Fenton told him, 'I want you to know that I would not come with you to High Wycombe.' As you may gather from that comment, life was not exactly easy travelling into the heart of Borneo.

In this extract, Redmond and James are journeying up the river with their guides, Dana, Leon and Inghai. After an accident in which Leon saves James Fenton from drowning, they come to the village of the Kenyah – a tribe of famous head-hunters. They are told there is to be a welcome party and are ushered into the long house, a communal room, and given the very potent alcoholic drink, tuak. The music starts and Redmond sits back to watch the show.

The chief's son entered, transformed. On his head he wore a war-helmet, a woven rattan cap set with black and yellow and crimson beads, topped with six long black and white plumes from the tail of the Helmeted hornbill. He was dressed in a war-coat, made from the skin of the largest cat in Borneo, the Clouded leopard. His head placed through an opening at the front of the skin, the bulk stretched down his back, and on to it were fastened row upon row of Rhinoceros hornbill feathers. Around his waist, slung on a silver belt and sheathed in a silver scabbard, was a parang to outshine all other parangs, its hilt intricately carved in horn from the antler of the kijang, the big Borneo deer. In his left hand, his arm crooked behind it, he carried a long shield, pointed at both ends, and from the centre of which a huge mask regarded us implacably, its eyes red, its teeth the painted tusks of the wild boar. Thick black tufts of hair hung in neat lines down either edge and across the top and bottom, tufts of hair which, we were led to believe, had long ago been taken from the scalps of heads cut off in battle.

Laying the ancient, and presumably fragile, shield carefully against the wall, the warrior took up his position at the centre of the floor. He crouched down and, at a nod from the man on the base string, a hollow, complicated, urgent, rhythmic music began. With exaggerated movements, his thigh muscles bunching and loosening, his tendons taut, a fierce concentration on his face, the chief's son turned slowly in time with the music, first on one foot and then on another, rising, inch by inch, to his own height, apparently peering over some imaginary cover. Sighting the enemy, he crouched again, and then, as the music quickened, he drew his bright parang and leapt violently forward, weaving and dodging, with immense exertion, cutting and striking, parrying unseen blows with his mimed shield. For a small second, his ghostly foe was off-guard, tripped on the shingle, and the heir to the Lordship of all the Kenyah of Nanga Sinyut claimed his victory with one malicious blow.

Everyone clapped and cheered, and so did I. Five young girls rushed forward to take off the hero's hornbill helmet, and war-coat, and parang. It was wonderful. The girls were very beautiful. All was right with the world. And then I realised, as a Rajah Brooke's birdwing took a flap around my duodenum, that the beautiful girls, in a troop, were coming, watched by all the longhouse, for me.

'You'll be all right,' said James, full of tuak. 'Just do your thing. Whatever it is.'

Strapped into the war-coat and the parang, the hornbill feathers on my head, I had a good idea. It would be a simple procedure to copy the basic steps that the chief's son had just shown us. There really was not much to it, after all. The music struck up, sounding just a little bit stranger than it had before.

I began the slow crouch on one leg, turning slightly. Perhaps, actually, this was a mistake, I decided. Ghastly pains ran up my thighs. Terminal cramp hit both buttocks at once. Some silly girl began to titter. A paraplegic wobble spread down my back. The silly girl began to laugh. Very slowly, the floor came up to say hello, and I lay down on it. There was uproar in the longhouse. How very funny, indeed.

Standing up, I reasoned that phase two would be easier. Peering over the imaginary boulder, I found myself looking straight into the eyes of an old man on the far side of the verandah. The old fool was crying with laughter, his ridiculous long ears waggling about. Drawing the parang, which was so badly aligned that it stuck in the belt and nearly took my fingers off, I advanced upon the foe, jumping this way and that, feeling dangerous. The old man fell off his seat. There was so much misplaced mirth, so much plain howling, that I could not hear the music, and so perhaps my rhythm was not quite right.

'Redsi!' came an unmistakable shout, 'why don't you improvise?'

Stabbed in the back just as I was about to take my very first head, I spun round violently to glare at the Fenton. I never actually saw him, because the cord of the war-helmet, not used to such movements, slipped up over the back of my head, and the helmet itself, flying forward, jammed fast over my face. Involuntarily, I took a deep gasp of its sweat-smooth rattan interior, of the hair of generations of Kenyah warriors who had each been desperate to impress the girls of their choice. It was an old and acrid smell.

The boards were shaking. The audience was out of control. And then, just in time, before suffocation set in, the five girls, grossly amused, set me free.

*from* Into the Heart of Borneo *by Redmond O'Hanlon*

## Group discussion

A book like *Into the Heart of Borneo*, in which two white men go in search of adventure and encounter 'primitive' tribes, risks being patronising towards the people it portrays; it could easily turn into a case of 'Let's all laugh at the funny natives!' Judging by the way this passage describes the Kenyah, do you think the book falls into this trap? Here are some questions to help you to focus your discussion:

(a)  How does Redmond come across?

(b)  How does Redmond describe the Kenyah? Look for adjectives and adverbs that describe them and their actions.

(c)  At whom do we laugh during the passage?

(d)  Do you think the Kenyah would be offended by their portrayal in this passage?

## Suggestions for writing

1  Although this is a humorous piece of writing, it has a serious side. Not only is the dancing powerful and beautiful, but O'Hanlon gives us the sense that the performances are part of a tradition that is still very much alive. When the chief's son dances, every movement carries meaning. How does this compare with our society in which most of our entertainment comes from television and radio? Write an essay in which you compare the dancing in the longhouse with Western forms of entertainment. Here are some questions to help you focus your thoughts:

(a)  Do we have our equivalents of the tribal dance in the disco and theatre?

(b)  Is television satisfactory as our main form of entertainment?

(c)  Our grandparents and great-grandparents say that before everyone had a TV they made their own entertainment. Are there any occasions when this is still true or has this practice died out?

(d)  If it has died out, are we missing anything?

(e) Do you think that the traditions of the Kenyah are likely to survive?

2  Redmond O'Hanlon's performance goes horribly wrong and he ends up making a fool of himself. Some of us, it seems, are born performers while others would rather never set foot on the stage. Write about your experiences of appearing on stage. What did it feel like to be in front of an audience? How did the audience react?

# THE FINAL CHOICE

After years of mountaineering, Joe Simpson and his friend Simon Yates decided to attempt the West Face of the Siula Grande in the Peruvian Andes. The ascent goes according to plan but on the way down Simpson falls and breaks his leg. His friend is lowering him down from ledge to ledge, past walls of ice, when disaster strikes.

The sense of weight on my harness increased, as did the speed. I tried braking with my arms but to no effect. I twisted round and looked up into the darkness. Rushes of snow flickered in my torch beam. I yelled for Simon to slow down. The speed increased, and my heart jumped wildly. Had he lost control? I tried braking again. Nothing. I stifled the rising panic and tried to think clearly – no, he hadn't lost control. I'm going down fast but it's steady. He's trying to be quick . . . that's all. I knew it to be true, but there was still something wrong.

It was the slope. Of course! I should have thought of it earlier. It was now much steeper, and that could mean only one thing – I was approaching another drop.

I screamed out a frantic warning but he couldn't hear me. I shouted again, as loud as I could, but the words were whipped away into the snow clouds. He wouldn't have heard me fifteen feet away. I tried to guess how far I was from the half-way knot. A hundred feet? Fifty? I had no idea. Each lowering became timeless. I slid for ever through the boiling snow without any sense of time passing – just a barely endurable period of agony.

A sense of great danger washed over me. I *had* to stop. I realised that Simon would hear nothing, so I must stop myself. If he felt my weight come off the rope he would know there must be a good reason. I grabbed my ice axe and tried to brake my descent. I leant heavily over the axe head, burying it in the slope, but it wouldn't bite. The snow was too loose. I dug my left boot into the slope but it, too, just scraped through the snow.

Then abruptly my feet were in space. I had time to cry out, and claw hopelessly at the snow before my whole body swung off an edge. I jerked on to the rope and toppled over backwards, spinning in circles from my harness. The rope ran up to a lip of ice and I saw that I was still descending. The sight vanished as a heavy avalanche of powder poured over me.

When it ceased I realised that I had stopped moving. Simon had managed to hold the impact of my body suddenly coming on to the rope. I was confused. I didn't understand what had happened, except that I was hanging free in space. I grabbed the rope and pulled myself up into a sitting position. The spinning continued but it was slowing down. I could see an ice wall six feet away from me every time I completed a spin. When I stopped spinning I was facing away from the wall and had to twist round to look at it. The spindrift had stopped. I shone my torch up the wall following the line of the rope until I could make out the edge I had gone over. It was about fifteen feet above me. The wall was solid ice and steeply overhanging. The rope jerked down a few inches, then stopped. Another avalanche of powder poured over the edge, and the wind blew it in eddies round me. I hunched protectively.

Looking between my legs, I could see the wall dropping below, angled away from me. It was overhanging all the way to the bottom. I stared down trying to judge the height of the wall. I thought I could see the snow-covered base of the wall with the dark outline of a crevasse directly beneath me, then snow flurries blocked my view. I looked back at the edge above. There was no chance of Simon hauling me up. It would have been extremely hard with a solid belay.* Sitting in the snow seat, it would be suicidal to attempt it. I shouted at the darkness

---

*Belay: a safe stance; to belay is to anchor safely to the mountain. A belay plate is a friction device used to control the rope in the event of a fall.

*Nick Estcourt, on expedition with Chris Bonnington, climbing a fixed rope on the south face of the Ogre, 1977.*

above and heard an unintelligible muffled yell. I couldn't be sure whether it had been Simon or an echo of my own shout.

I waited silently, hugging the rope with my arms to stay upright, and feeling shocked as I stared between my legs at the drop. Gradually, and with a sense of mounting dread, I began to get some perspective into what I was looking at. I was an awfully long way above the crevasse at the base of the cliff, and as it slowly dawned on me I felt my stomach lurch with fear. There was at least 100 feet of air below my feet! I kept staring at the drop, hoping to find I was mistaken. I realised that, far from being wrong, I had been conservative in my estimate. For a moment I did nothing while my thoughts whirled and I tried to assess how things had changed. Then one fact jolted through my thoughts.

I swung round and stared at the wall. It was six feet from me. At full arm's reach, I still couldn't reach the ice with my axe. I tried swinging towards the wall but ended up spinning help-lessly. I knew that I had to get back up the rope, and I had to do it quickly: Simon had no idea what I'd gone over. The other steep drops were short walls. He had no reason to assume this would be any different. In that case he might lower me. Oh,

Jesus, I'll jam on the half-way knot long before I get to the bottom!

It was impossible to reach the wall, and I realised quickly that it wouldn't help me. I couldn't climb fifteen feet of overhanging ice with one leg. I fumbled at my waist for the two loops of rope I had tied there. I found them but couldn't grip them with my mitts on. I wrenched off the mitts with my teeth and reached for the two loops again. I slipped one over my wrist and held the second in my teeth. In reaching for the loops I had let go of the rope and tumbled over backwards so that I hung from the waist. My rucksack had pulled me over, and I hung in an inverted curve with my head and legs lower than my waist. I struggled to swing up until I reached the rope and pulled myself back to a sitting position.

I crooked my left arm around the rope to hold me upright, and took the loop from my teeth with my right hand. I tried to twist the thin loop of cord around the rope but my fingers were too numbed. I needed to get a Prussik knot on to the rope, so that I could slide the knot up and hang in tension as the knot tightened. The effort of holding myself up was exhausting. At last, using a combination of teeth and hand, I managed to twist the loop around the rope, and then tried repeating the process. I needed at least three twists before the knot would be of any use. By the time I had succeeded I was almost crying with frustration. It had taken me nearly fifteen minutes. The wind nudged me into a gentle spin and blasted the incessant avalanches into my face, blinding me. I clipped a karabiner into the Prussik loop and fastened it to my waist.

I shoved the loop as far up the rope as I could reach and leant back on it. The knot tightened, slipped a few inches, and then held me. I let go of the rope and hung back. I remained sitting up. The second loop had to be tied on to the rope but this time I would be able to use both hands.

It wasn't until I tried to slip it off my left wrist that I realised how useless my hands were. Both were frozen. I could move the fingers of my right hand, but my left hand, which had been still as I held on to the rope, had seized. I thumped them together, bending the fingers in against my palms. I hit them, bent them, hit them, again and again, but there were no hot aches. Some movement and feeling returned but it was minimal.

I took the loop from my wrist and held it against the rope. At my first attempt to twist it around and back inside itself I dropped it. It fell on to the main rope knot on my harness and I grabbed at it before it was blown off. Then, as I lifted it to the rope, it seemed to slide out of my hand. I grabbed at it with my left hand and managed to catch it against my right forearm. I couldn't pick it up. My fingers refused to close round it, and as I tried slipping it up my arm it dropped again. This time I watched it fall away beneath me. I knew at once that I now had no chance of climbing up the rope. It would have been hard enough doing it with two loops, and now, with both hands so useless, I had no chance. I slumped on to the rope and swore bitterly.

At least I wasn't having to hold myself up. It was a consolation although I knew it achieved little else. The rope ran up from my waist taut as an iron bar. The loop I had attached gripped the rope three feet above my harness. I unclipped it from my harness and then threaded it through my rucksack straps so that it pulled them together across my chest. I fastened it with my last karabiner and leant back to test it. The effect was good. The loop now held my torso up on the rope so that I sat in space as if in an armchair. When I was sure it was as good as I could get it, I slumped back on to the rope feeling utterly weary.

The wind gusted against me, making me swing crazily on the rope, and with each gust I was getting colder. The pressure of the harness on my waist and thighs had cut off the circulation and both legs felt numb. The pain in the knee had gone. I let my arms hang slackly, feeling the deadweight of useless hands in my mitts. There was no point in reviving them. There was no way out of this slow hanging. I couldn't go up, and Simon would never get me down. I tried to work out how long it had been since I had gone over the edge. I decided it could be no more than half an hour. In two hours I would be dead. I could feel the cold taking me.

When Joe Simpson decided to write about his ordeal he asked Simon Yates what his thoughts had been during the descent. In the finished book, these appear in italics at various points in the narrative. Simon now takes up the story.

*It had been nearly an hour since Joe had gone over the drop. I was shaking with cold. My grip on the rope kept easing despite my efforts. The rope slowly edged down and the knot pressed against my right fist. I can't hold it, can't stop it. The thought overwhelmed me. The snow slides and wind and cold were forgotten. I was being pulled off. The seat moved beneath me, and snow slipped away past my feet. I slipped a few inches. Stamping my feet deep into the slope halted the movement. God! I had to do something!*

*The knife! The thought came out of nowhere. Of course, the knife. Be quick, come on, get it.*

*The knife was in my sack. It took an age to let go a hand and slip the strap off my shoulder, and then repeat it with the other hand. I braced the rope across my thigh and held on to the plate with my right hand as hard as I could. Fumbling at the catches on the rucksack, I could feel the snow slowly giving way beneath me. Panic threatened to swamp me. I felt in the sack, searching desperately for the knife. My hand closed round something smooth and I pulled it out. The red plastic handle slipped in my mitt and I nearly dropped it. I put it in my lap before tugging my mitt off with my teeth. I had already made the decision. There was no other option left to me. The metal blade stuck to my lips when I opened it with my teeth.*

*I reached down to the rope and then stopped. The slack rope! Clear the loose rope twisted round my foot! If it tangled it would rip me down with it. I carefully cleared it to one side, and checked that it all lay in the seat away from the belay plate. I reached down again, and this time I touched the blade to the rope.*

*It needed no pressure. The taut rope exploded at the touch of the blade, and I flew backwards into the seat as the pulling strain vanished. I was shaking.*

*Leaning back against the snow, I listened to a furious hammering in my temple as I tried to calm my breathing. Snow hissed over me in a torrent. I ignored it as it poured over my face and chest, spurting into the open zip at my neck, and on down below. It kept coming. Washing across me and down after the cut rope, and after Joe.*

*I was alive, and for the moment that was all I could think about. Where Joe was, or whether he was alive, didn't concern me in the long silence after the cutting. His weight had gone from me. There was only the wind and the avalanches left to me.*

*from* Touching the Void *by Joe Simpson*

# Group discussion

Of course, Joe and Simon both lived to tell the harrowing story of their mountain descent but their brush with death raises an important question: why do many men and women risk their lives doing dangerous things like climbing mountains? To help you discuss this, think about the following:

(a) Have you ever done anything dangerous? If so, how did you feel?
(b) Do dangerous activities attract a certain type of person?
(c) What do people gain from risking their lives?

# Suggestions for writing

1 Later in the book, when Simon and Joe are re-united, Simon admits that he had been sure that Joe was dead (he even burnt his clothes) and that he was responsible. As he descends the mountain alone, Simon keeps thinking about how he is going to break the news to Joe's mother – 'I'm sorry, Mrs Simpson, but I had to cut the rope. . . . She'd never understand, never believe me . . .'. Write an imaginary version of this conversation from Simon's point of view. Start your writing as Simon walks down the road towards Mrs Simpson's house. What is he thinking? How might Mrs Simpson react? Concentrate on building up atmosphere, detailing every fluctuation in her expression and Simon's feelings.

2 The whole episode narrated in this extract did not last much more than an hour and yet it seems to go on for ever. For some reason, during awful moments time seems almost to stand still. When we look back on such times it is often the tiny details that we remember. Using *The Final Choice* as a guide, write an imaginary account of a life and death incident. Concentrate on achieving the slow-motion quality of the two extracts. Here are some ideas to help you:

- A survivor describes a plane or car crash.
- A cashier describes an armed robbery.
- A soldier describes a battle.

Remember, it is the small details that make an impact in times of stress. Try as hard as you can to imagine yourself in such a situation and write about what you see, hear and feel.

OR

You may have experienced something like this yourself (being involved in an accident, for instance). If so, write about it in as much detail as you can remember. Try to make your readers experience the pain and fear that you felt and the tremendous feeling of relief when you realised that you had survived.

# *Extensions*

The extracts used in this unit are from the following books:

*In the Ditch* by Buchi Emecheta (Flamingo/Pan, 1973)
*Inside Out* by Rosie Johnston (Michael Joseph, 1989)
*Under a Crescent Moon* by Daniel De Souza (Serpent's Tail, 1989)
*Into the Heart of Borneo* by Redmond O'Hanlon (Penguin, 1985)
*Touching the Void* by Joe Simpson (Cape, 1988)
'White into Black' by Martha Gellhorn is taken from the magazine
*GRANTA*.

1 If you enjoyed reading the extracts from *Into the Heart of Borneo*
   and 'White into Black' then you might like to read some more travel
   writing. Here are some travel books that GCSE and Standard Grade
   students have enjoyed:
   *The Great Railway Bazaar* by Paul Theroux (Penguin)
   *In Patagonia* by Bruce Chatwin (Picador)
   *A Time of Gifts* by Patrick Leigh Fermor (Penguin)
   *A Traveller's Life* by Eric Newby (Picador)
   *The Valley of the Assassins* by Freya Stark (Century)
   *Not a Hazardous Sport* by Nigel Barley (Penguin)
   You could write a very interesting open study or project comparing
   two or three of these books.

2 If you enjoyed reading the extracts from *Under a Crescent Moon*, by
   Daniel De Souza and *Inside Out* by Rosie Johnston then you could
   read these books and compare them to other prison writings. Here
   are some books you could try – they are not as depressing as you
   might think! All the following books are by people who have
   struggled through the pain of prison life towards a greater freedom.

   *Grey is the Colour of Hope* by Irina Ratushinskaya (Hodder and
   Stoughton)
   *Pain of Confinement* by Jimmy Boyle (Pan)
   *Labelled a Black Villain* by Trevor Hercules (Fourth Estate)
   *Knockback* by Peter Adams and Shirley Cooklin (Ariel)
   *Prisoner Without a Name, Cell Without a Number* by Jacobo
   Timerman (Penguin)

3 If you found Buchi Emecheta's account of life in Pussy Cat Mansions
   interesting then why not read the whole of *In the Ditch* (and her
   'prequel' *Second Class Citizen*) and compare it with a novel on the
   same theme by the West Indian writer Samuel Selvon, *The Lonely
   Londoners*.

# 4 SEEING, HEARING, WRITING

Description plays a part in almost every kind of writing; in stories, autobiography, even to some extent in discursive essays when you wish to illustrate a point. The three writers discussed in this Unit, however, have chosen to write pieces of prose that are purely descriptive. They have no function other than to allow the reader to see and hear exactly what the writer has seen and heard.

The first extract is taken from Bella Chagall's memoir of her childhood in pre-revolutionary Russia, *Burning Lights*. In this piece she guides us around her father's jewellery shop.

# THE SHOP

A quite different world opens before me when I only just push at the heavy door that separates the shop from our apartment.

It is a door entirely covered with tin. Instead of a latch it has a big key that is always in the lock. In the dark rear shop, into which I tumble first, I grope along the walls as though I were blind. Thick yellow sheets of paper rustle underfoot.

Wrapped-up wall clocks rest on the floor here. Until they are hung on walls, they do not move; they lie quiet and soundless, as if buried alive. But the stuffy air of the dark chamber seems swollen with the voices that seep in from the shop. The voices crowd against the high wooden wall and recoil from it again. I stand behind it as in a prison, and listen to what is being said. I want to make out whose voice is talking. And if I catch mother's voice, I am content.

But wait! Is her voice quiet, calm, or, God forbid, angry? Mother's voice will give me warning, tell me whether to go into the shop or not.

Her high tones encourage me. I touch the curtain of the last door, which leads to the shop. I become dizzy at once because of the mirrors and glass. All the clocks are being wound in my ears. The shop is full of glitter on every side. The flashing of silver and gold blinds me like fire; it is reflected in the mirrors, roams over the glass drawers. It dazzles my eyes.

Two large gas chandeliers burn high up under the ceiling, humming loudly; the second becomes a moan of pain. Fire spatters from the close-netted caps on the burners that barely hold back the sparks.

There are two high walls entirely lined from top to bottom with glass cupboards. The cupboards reach up to the ceiling and are so solidly built that they seem to have grown into it. Their glass doors slide easily back and forth. Through the glass one can clearly see all the objects on display, almost touch them with one's hand.

On the shelves are goblets, wineglasses, sugar bowls, saucers, braided baskets, milk and water pitchers, boxes for etrogim, fruit bowls. Everything shines and glitters with a newly polished look. Whenever I move, all the objects run after me in reflection. The fire of the lamps and the light of the silver cross each other. Now the silver drowns in a flash of the lamplight, now it re-emerges with an even sharper glitter.

On the opposite wall there is another glass cupboard. Behind its panes are objects not of silver but of white metal, and their gleam is much more modest, and quieter.

In the center of the shop, on three sides, there rise, as if from the floor itself, three inner walls – long counters with drawers. They divide the shop into two sections. All laid out with glass, full of gold objects, they glitter like magical arks. Little stones of all colors, framed in gold rings, earrings, brooches, bracelets, flicker there like lighted matches.

In this air full of fire it is quite impossible to see that the floor is dark. At the front, at the very feet of the customers, entire silver services shine through the glass. And so even the customers' black shoes glitter and catch reflections along with the silver.

The third wall is dim even by day. Overgrown with long hanging clocks, it looks like a forest of dark trees. There are wall clocks of various sizes. Some have big, squat cases with thick hanging chains supporting heavy copper weights. Other wall clocks have narrower, slimmer bodies. Their chains are lighter, more movable, with smaller weights attached. In the bellies of all of them pointed pendulums dangle like swords, swinging restlessly back and forth.

Among the large wall clocks smaller ones are hiding, and even tiny ones; one can see only the white dials, their round moon faces. They have no wooden bellies, and their chain legs move in the open, before everyone's eyes, up and down.

The whole wall of clocks sighs and breathes heavily. From each box come smothered groans, as though at every moment someone were being killed on the dark wall.

Suddenly I begin to quake. One of the heavy clocks awakens, and, like an old man rousing, it utters such a groan that I look around quickly to see whether its body has fallen apart.

Heavily it strikes the hours. My heart pounds with its heart. And I am glad when the minute hand moves away a bit from the hour hand, giving me time to catch my breath before the old thing utters another groan.

Another clock acts as though it were blowing its nose, or hoarsely rending its throat in broken laughter.

In contrast, the little clocks have high, thin little voices. They wail like children awakened in terror in the middle of the night.

The clocks move, their pendulums swing, for days and nights on end. When do they rest?

Suddenly several clocks together begin to chime. Do they do it on purpose, in order not to let me hear how each one sounds by itself?

I turn my head from one clock to another. I am bewildered. I hear voices that seem to come straight from the earth.

These are the little alarm clocks lying on the floor in cardboard boxes. Like clamoring brats they awaken the old wall clocks.

I rush to twist their little heads in order to make them stop yelling. But I stop halfway. My heart melts. A gentle song rises on the air. I know that it is a music box that is singing. I quickly open its lid. The song flies out like a bird from its nest. In the box there surges a sea of little wires, springs, wheels. Like waves they lift tiny millstones, jump over them, quickly run down, swim in the melody as in the current of a stream. Each little spring, each little wheel breaks into sound. They hum the melody till they lose their breath.

I go quite close to the music box; I want to assure it that someone is listening, that it must not stop playing. But suddenly the little wheels stop. I do not close the lid. I wait – perhaps it will want to sing again.

Such a warm world has risen from the dark one and spread over the whole shop! Even the wall clocks are holding their breath.

Every night, before going to sleep, one of my brothers goes to have a look at the shop. My parents send him to see whether everything is in order, whether, God forbid, a burglar has not broken in. I too want to see how all the objects on display sleep there at night.

As soon as the big key of the metal door creaks, I shudder. I am afraid to go there, even with my brother. What if the angel of death with all his devils were concealed there?

But they have a little light. A small table lamp burns there overnight. The wick is twisted. The smoke of the smothered flame drags out our shadows, whirls them before my eyes.

A smoky veil covers also the wall with the shelves of silver. Only here and there, a sleepy eye seems to open – a carved flower sparkles, a raised ornament flickers; suddenly a full glow of silver light shines forth, like the moon rolling out from behind the clouds.

I am afraid to go closer to the wall of the clocks. They hang on black nails, as though eternally crucified. It seems to me that open graves sigh there. The clocks are barely moving, their pendulums drag like limping feet. The white dials with their black dots wink with faded eyes, like specters.

I heard them from a distance and help them to sigh. It seems to me that they are calling me, that they are prodding me in the back. With a heavy heart I leave them.

I see that in our apartment, in our dining room, there is also a wall clock, but it is enclosed inside a high, carved cabinet. One does not hear its heart pound, one does not see its outstretched legs. It strikes the hours with a muffled tone that has no spirit.

*from* Burning Lights *by Bella Chagall*

## Group discussion

- Now that you have read the piece, if you look closely you will see that some parts of the writing give an impression of light and others of darkness. In your group, decide which are the light sections and which are the dark ones.

- Now discuss these questions:
  (a)  What feelings does Chagall associate with the dark and the light?
  (b)  What kind of pattern does this use of contrasts give the passage?
  (c)  How does Chagall create the impression that this is a child's eye view of the shop?

## Suggestions for writing

1  It is as if Bella Chagall takes us by the hand and leads us around her father's shop. This technique allows her to describe each element of the room in turn. Try using the same method yourself in your own description of a room that you know well. You could also adopt Bella Chagall's way of using the patterns of light and dark in the room to add an emotional dimension to your writing.

2  Write descriptions of four rooms either from memory or from your imagination. Choose the rooms so that they contrast with one another. For instance, the first one might be a room in a squat and the next the drawing-room of a stately home.

Do not include any people in your writing. The test of a good description will be if your reader can guess what sort of people might be connected with the room.

# DIARY 1964–85

Ian Breakwell is a painter who has been keeping an unusual diary for the last 20 years. This diary does not record his thoughts and feelings; instead, in it he describes the fragments of everyday street life that he encounters. Of course, the things that Ian Breakwell writes about are going on around us all the time but we have not trained ourselves to notice them.

The following diary entries are typical of Ian Breakwell's technique. He walks around with his eyes open and sets down what he sees with great clarity; just like verbal snapshots.

**26.8.1977**   London: Smithfield Market, 9.30 am

I was finishing my breakfast when there was a knock on the door. A black man was staring through the window. I opened the door. He stood silently and handed me a slip of paper on which were written the words: 'MISS JEAN.' I said I did not understand. His mouth opened wide but no sound came out. I realized he was dumb. Possibly deaf as well. He handed me the slip of paper again: 'MISS JEAN.' I handed it back. His eyes bulged and he began to make imploring gestures with his hands. I said: 'I don't think I can help you.' I wrote it down on the piece of paper: 'I DO NOT THINK I CAN HELP YOU. I DO NOT KNOW MISS JEAN. SORRY.' He went back down the stairs, a look of abject despair on his face.

Moorgate Underground Station, 10.15 am

I am sitting on a bench on the platform glancing at my watch.

No sign of a train. I'm going to be late. A neat, anonymous man in a grey raincoat sits down next to me and says: 'Why do you rush from place to place? Your face is tense, you are thin and worried, you are driving yourself into the ground. Remember you only live twice. I used to rush around like you and I worked myself into an early grave. Then I took stock of myself, and since I returned to earth I have maintained a steady course. I learnt my lesson.'

**29.8.1977**   London: Smithfield Gardens, 11 am

The moment when the clock struck; the sun burst through the clouds; the shadow of the statue with its pointing finger raced across the ground; the five pigeons stood poised in a line, each with its right foot raised; a shiver ran down the back of my neck before my eyes shut tight.

[. . .]

**3.2.1978**   Leeds: Merrion Centre, 10.23 am

Two television sets side by side in a shop window: on one screen a pile of corpses in Auschwitz; on the other screen a smiling housewife putting a joint of pork into the oven. Behind one television set a shop assistant manicuring her nails; behind the other television set a man picking his teeth with a matchstick.

**23.2.1978**   Glasgow: St George's Square, 2.50 pm

A man playing a harmonica and walking along the pavement just too fast for people to put any coins in the cap which he holds in his outstretched hand.

Glasgow: Kelvingrove, 11.45 pm

The empty street glistening in the pouring rain. The sound of footsteps on the pavement of a side street. A television set in the window of a house facing onto the street; on screen a window through which can be seen the footprints of webbed feet; in the background a man clutching his throat, his eyes bulging.

**10.3.1978**   London

In the dentist's waiting room the patients sit smiling bravely. From the other side of the wall comes the whine of the electric drill. Through the half-open door of the surgery can be seen a woman's quivering legs stretched out in the chair. The door closes, then one minute later opens again. The dentist's assistant, a girl with coal-black hair and eyes, strides out of the surgery carrying a long-handled drain plunger. She smiles and says: 'There, that should do the trick.'

[. . .]

**15.4.1983** Norwich, 9.30 am

The gales and cold, lashing rain have disappeared overnight and half-timbered Norwich is bathed in glorious sunshine like a picture postcard. I pedal over to the outdoor market and sit in the sun on a bench eating hot bacon rolls with a cup of tea. On an adjoining bench two lovers are having a tiff. He sits stony-faced, his arms crossed, ignoring her tearful reproaches. She stands forlorn, looking at the ground, then walks away. He continues to sit staring grimly, arms folded. A few minutes later she returns with a red rose she has bought from the market which she places on his lap, then puts her arms round his neck and kisses him on his cheek. He allows her to do so. They get up and leave, he with his hands thrust into his jacket pockets, her with her arm through his. She looks up at him. He looks straight ahead, a little smile of smug satisfaction on his otherwise stern face.

*Ian Breakwell*

## Group discussion

What kind of language does Ian Breakwell use? Look carefully at each entry and discuss the following:

(a) Does he use a large number of descriptive words (adjectives and adverbs)?

(b) Would you describe the vocabulary as simple or difficult?

(c) Which tense does he use?

(d) Are the sentences long or short? How are they punctuated?

(e) Does he use colours?

(f) Are there any similies (using 'like' or 'as')?

When you have the answers to these questions, discuss how vocabulary, tense and sentence structure contribute to the effectiveness of the writing.

## Suggestion for writing

1 One of the ways Breakwell achieves his effects is through the juxtaposition of images; that is to say that what is important about his

writing is the way that he places one description alongside another (the two television pictures, for instance in the entry for 3.2.78). This makes his writing very much like poetry.

Try using the TV shop idea yourself. Write a poem based on a description of a TV shop window in which the televisions are each showing a different image. Choose the images carefully so that the contrasts tell us something about our society.

**2** Some of Breakwell's diary entries seem to hint at a story behind the simple descriptions. Use one of the entries as the basis for a story of your own in which you develop the characters and relationships hinted at by Ian Breakwell. The last entry would probably be the most suitable.

Now compare Ian Breakwell's style with the writing of John Berger in the following extracts from 'On The Edge of a Foreign City'. As you will see, Berger uses a similar technique but the effect is subtlety different.

# ON THE EDGE OF A FOREIGN CITY

In these three descriptions John Berger attempts to put the scene before his eyes into words. However, unlike Ian Breakwell, he does not only describe each scene. He uses his imagination to 'read' the actions and the expressions of the people to interpret what he sees.

Outside the cathedral of St Jean many cars and two buses are parked: men are in their shirtsleeves. It is Sunday morning when the croissants have more butter in them.

Inside it is crowded. All the chairs are taken and the aisles are full of people standing. It is unusual to see a church so full in this country. But as we make our way forward, towards the priests, the explanation becomes clear. In the centre of the church, surrounded and hidden on three sides by the rest of the congregation and on the fourth side facing the carpeted steps leading up to the high altar, is a square of a hundred girls in white. The white of their long dresses, the white of their gloves and the white of their veils is spotless and uncrumpled. At home a hundred irons must still be warm.

The girls are between eleven and thirteen years old. Against the white their faces look nut-brown. They are caught between the questions and responses which they exchange with the priest and the gaze of their parents and guardians who are in the front ranks of the surrounding congregation and who watch their every move. Caught like this, they seem very still: and, having forgone their freedom of independent movement, very peaceful.

It is somewhat like watching children who are asleep. To the eye of the watcher they acquire a false innocence. In fact if one watches carefully enough, one can distinguish between various degrees of experience. Some are only pretending to sleep and in their white shoes wriggle their toes until they can say what they are dying to say to their companions. Out of the corner of their eyes they have observed the remarkable behaviour of the widow who is watching her niece and constantly smooths down her own black dress over her old hips with thin hands – thirty times a minute.

Some are so aware of what they are wearing, so aware of the white which draws the eyes of all who surround them, that they have begun to dream of getting married.

A few feel impure before the shining purity of the recipient of their vows, and on the faces of these there is a kind of beatitude – as there is in the sight of a white sail so far away that the hull of the ship is invisible.

There is one girl who is a little taller than most of the others and among the nearest to us. She has an aquiline nose and large, dark eyes. Her veil is so crisp that it looks like a linen napkin. Her family are perhaps richer than those of the others. She is proud and self-possessed – as though, if she were sleeping, she would sleep in exactly the position she had decided upon. For her the religious experience which she is now undergoing is part of her private plan for her own development. It is no seduction. It is a long-arranged engagement. But none the less intense. All that will be done unto her will be done in the way that she selects. Always provided that no disaster occurs so that her wishes and decisions become incidental, her life no more than a movement which catches a sniper's eye.

By the west door the man who sells tracts sits behind his table and reads a newspaper.

The girls as they answer sound like doves.

Some of their mothers, pressed right forward to the front rank round the square of girls, have to restrain themselves from putting out a hand and touching their daughters. Their excuse for doing this would be the smoothing of a dress, the straightening of a cuff. But their desire to do so comes from the need to share their memories. They want at this moment to touch their daughters not because their daughters might need their support, but because they want their daughters to know that twenty years ago they too were confirmed in white dresses.

The men stand further back: as though the degree of proximity were inversely related to the degree of scepticism. They watch a ceremony. One or two consult their watches. All are dwarfed by the vast height of the piers. After the ceremony they will go to cafés and restaurants to celebrate. This evening some will play bowls. For many scepticism is mixed with calculation. If their daughters' being received into the church offers in one way or another the possibility of their children being better protected, then indeed they are glad that at last it has come to this – their confirmation. Caution fills their souls.

[. . .]

An hour's drive from the centre is a mountain. It is 1,800 metres high. In the hollows are small patches of frozen snow, over which children slide and toboggan on rubber mats – this even in June.

None of the ascents is steep or dangerous. If they take their time, quite elderly couples can walk to the summit.

Today is Sunday and there must be 3,000 people on this mountain.

The road stops a few hundred metres from the top. On the grass – springy as only grass that is several months of the year under snow can be – the cars and a bus are parked. In the evening when they are all gone, the hill looks like any other. There are no kiosks or litter bins. Only the grass that owes its special nature to the snow.

At the summit there are a few rocks. Otherwise the sides are all grass, and among the grass are mountain flowers: gentian, arnica, mountain anemones – and thousands of jonquils.

It is possible to scramble up the mountain from any direction, but there is a path which takes the easiest route. Along this path there is a constant traffic of couples, fathers carrying babies, grandparents, schoolchildren. Many of them are barefoot. From below, the procession, ascending and descending, looks a little like a medieval vision of some exchange with heaven. The more so because most of those coming down are carrying armfuls of jonquils, white-gold in colour.

From the summit one can see the ranges extending to the horizon. The rock joins with the sky and their common blue discounts every difference.

Towards the south one can also see the plain, intensely culti-vated, the colour of greengages. Such a view is archetypal. It is the antithesis of a view of the grave.

Across the plain moves the shadow of one white cloud. Where the shadow is, the green is the green of laurel leaves.

The crowd, which is made up of hundreds of dispersed groups, is easy and at home. It is as if the mountain were their common ancestor.

[. . .]

Today there was a woman being bundled into a taxi: but she refused to bend her back, so she wouldn't fit inside the door. There were two men struggling with her. Quite respectable middle-aged men steeling themselves in righteousness against the doubting eyes of the crowd that had gathered. Then the woman began to shout. I couldn't understand a word. But she shouted in such a way that it was obvious she believed that across the street, somewhere near where I was standing, there was somebody who understood what she was suffering and the reasonableness of her simple wish not to be bundled into the car and taken somewhere else. After several minutes' struggling the two men gave up: she wouldn't fit through the door. So they took her back, still shouting, and her knees bent as they dragged her along – she was only a woman of about forty-five – to the chemist's shop where they had originally been. Inside the shop she still fought, and one of the men had to stand with his back against the glass door to prevent her running out and away. It appeared that the chemist was trying to help them calm her. The taxi driver waited, the door of his taxi still open. Because one of the men was leaning with his back against the door, no customer could enter the shop. I watched through the window. There were the drugs and the medicines on the shelves. There was the woman with her will, that would have done what she wanted done and would prevent what she did not want. And between the shelves and the woman there were the men, hesitating.

*from* The White Bird *by John Berger*

## Group discussion

- How does Berger use language to achieve his effects? Read each extract carefully and discuss these questions:

  (a)   Does he use a large number of adjectives and adverbs?

  (b)   Would you describe his vocabulary as simple or difficult?

  (c)   Which tenses does he use?

  (d)   Are the sentences long or short?

  (e)   Does his language vary or are all three extracts similar in style?

(f)   Can you find examples of these techniques:

– repetition of words or phrases
– impersonal constructions (it may be . . . it seems that . . . one can feel . . .)
– simile (using 'like' or 'as')?

(g)   Does he describe colours?

When you have answered these questions, compare John Berger's use of language with Ian Breakwell's.

- Each section of 'On the Edge of a Foreign City' has its own atmosphere. Read each description through carefully. In your group, decide which of the following words best fit each piece. You may use each word more than once.

| | |
|---|---|
| love | hope |
| faith | suffering |
| fear | freedom |
| calm | captivity |
| panic | serenity |
| anger | beauty |
| happiness | peace |

You may add words of your own if you feel that the list does not include the word you want. Compare your decisions with those of other groups. Do you all agree?

## Suggestions for writing

1 Use one of Berger's descriptions as the basis for a story that deals with what leads up to the events he describes or what happens afterwards (for instance, mother and daughter dressing before the confirmation). The first and third extracts would probably be the most suitable for this treatment, but you could try using the second extract if you have a good idea for it.

2 Write one or two descriptions of your own of a scene either from memory or from your imagination. Each piece of writing must represent one or more of the words used in the discussion activity above (hope, for example, or freedom and beauty). In your writing, try to describe the scene in such away that it defines the word or words you have chosen.

3 Of course, Breakwell and Berger write their descriptions from real life, so why not try this yourself? Use Breakwell's *Diary* and 'On the Edge of a Foreign City' as models for your own pieces of descriptive writing.

## John Berger's method

This involves quite long and detailed accounts of unusual or striking scenes. To get the right effect, you will have to go out and search for interesting scenes. You will need to think just as you would if you were sketching a scene for your art coursework, except, of course, you will be using words instead of pictures.

You could try this technique in and around school. Although school life might appear humdrum there are, in fact, plenty of opportunities for catching staff and pupils in quite dramatic situations and there are always enough people around to enable you to observe them unobtrusively. Here are some examples of suitable places: an assembly, a lesson (remember always to get permission from whoever is taking these), a dining-room, the library, the playground at break.

If you decide to look further afield here are some helpful hints:

- Look for scenes that involve people. Cafés and parks are good, or try social events like weddings, prize-givings, etc.
- Don't attempt to write everything down while you are there. Just make some notes and then write them up at home.
- If you go with a friend don't look at your friend's work until yours is finished. It is important that your work is individual.
- Your choice of words is crucial so you will need to draft and re-draft your pieces until you are satisfied.
- Do not make each piece too long. Two sides of A4 should be the maximum for each description.
- Don't be tempted to cheat and write only from your imagination. Remember, fact is often stranger than fiction and your work is bound to be more interesting if it is based on observation.

## Ian Breakwell's method

Like Ian Breakwell, you could describe one or two scenes per day. This method depends more on your ability to observe than on your skill as a writer. You will need to keep your eyes open for suitable scenes during the day, rather like a photographer looking for good shots. The effectiveness of your writing will depend on your having picked the right scenes to describe. Remember, the world is full of people and action – all you have to do is to observe and describe.

Another way of working is to go out with a camera and take photos of scenes that interest you. When you get all your pictures developed, pick the most effective ones and describe them in words. This kind of project can lead to some interesting writing about your local area and its inhabitants; for instance, you could also write some stories or poems based around the people and places in your photos.

# *Extensions*

The extracts used in this unit come from:

*Burning Lights* by Bella Chagal (Schocken Books, 1962)
Ian Breakwell's *Diary 1964–1985* (Pluto Press, 1986)
*The White Bird* by John Berger (Chatto & Windus, 1988)

1  As part of your work on this unit, you could compile an anthology of effective descriptive writing. Include examples from fiction and non-fiction. When you have assembled all the extracts, write an introduction in which you explain why you have chosen each piece and what you find especially effective about it. Here is a list of writers generally considered to have great powers of observation and description. Your teacher will undoubtedly be able to add others.

   Charles Dickens (any of the novels – try the opening of *Bleak House*, for instance)
   George Orwell (*Down and Out in London and Paris*)
   Susan Hill (*I'm the King of the Castle* – try the description of Hang Wood)
   Thomas Hardy (any of the novels but especially the descriptions of Egdon Heath in *The Return of the Native*)
   William Golding (*Lord of the Flies*)
   Patrick Leigh Fermor (any of his travel books)
   Colin Thubron (travel books)

   Or look through Units One, Two and Three of this anthology – they contain plenty of examples of powerful description.

2  Normally, if you are asked to write a story, you probably think about the characters or plot first. Why not try a story in which the setting is as important as the characters?

   If you want to read a good example of this kind of writing, have a look at 'My Girl and the City' by Samuel Selvon, in which the central character explores London with his girlfriend. You can find it in *Best West Indian Stories* (ed. Ramchand, Nelson).

# 5 INVESTIGATIONS

We rely on journalists to be our eyes and ears; to describe to us experiences that we can never undergo ourselves. So we expect them to search out the truth and to present it to us as clearly as possible.

This unit contains the writing of journalists who have decided to investigate a particular subject and to set down what they see as the truth of the matter.

We are taken by Hanif Kureishi to Bradford where he asks the question – does this city tell us something about England as a whole?

'Last Days on Death Row', by film-maker Paul Hamann, describes the desperate attempts made to save the life of a prisoner who has been sentenced to death.

Polly Toynbee spends a frustrating day with a training officer and writes about her impressions in 'Girls' Careers'.

'It seems like the sky falls in' is taken from a book published by a group researching into the use of hard drugs. In this extract we find out how people have been affected by the discovery that someone in their family is addicted to heroin.

Gloria Steinem goes 'undercover' to become a Playboy Bunny and discovers that it is not as glamorous as it is cracked up to be.

# Investigation one
# BRADFORD

The first thing you notice as you get on the Inter-City train to Bradford is that the first three carriages are first class. These are followed by the first-class restaurant car. Then you are free to sit down. But if the train is packed and you cannot find an empty seat, you have to stand. You stand for the whole journey, with other people lying on the floor around you, and you look through at the empty seats in the first-class carriages where men sit in their shirt-sleeves doing important work and not looking up. The ticket collector has to climb over us to get to them.

Like the porters on the station, the ticket collector was black, probably of West Indian origin. In other words, black British. Most of the men fixing the railway line, in their luminous orange jackets, with pickaxes over their shoulders, were also black. The guard on the train was Pakistani, or should I say another Briton, probably born here, and therefore 'black'.

When I got to Bradford I took a taxi. It was simple: Bradford is full of taxis. Raise an arm and three taxis rush at you. Like most taxi drivers in Bradford, the driver was Asian and his car had furry, bright purple seats, covered with the kind of material people in the suburbs sometimes put on the lids of their toilets. It smelled of perfume, and Indian music was playing. The taxi driver had a Bradford-Pakistani accent, a cross between the north of England and Lahore, which sounds odd the first few times you hear it. Mentioning the accent irritates people in Bradford. How else do you expect people to talk? they say. And they are right. But hearing it for the first time disconcerted me because I found that I associated northern accents with white faces, with people who eat puddings, with Geoffrey Boycott and Roy Hattersley.

We drove up a steep hill, which overlooked the city. In the distance there were modern buildings and among them the older mill chimneys and factories with boarded-up windows. We passed Priestley Road. J. B. Priestley was born in Bradford, and in the early sixties both John Braine and Alan Sillitoe set novels here. I wondered what the writing of the next fifteen years would be like. There were, I was to learn, stories in abundance to be told.

The previous day I had watched one of my favourite films, Keith Waterhouse and Willis Hall's *Billy Liar*, also written in the early sixties. Billy works for an undertaker and there is a scene in which Billy tries to seduce one of his old girlfriends in a graveyard. Now I passed that old graveyard. It was full of monstrous mausoleums, some with spires thirty feet high; others were works of architecture in themselves, with arches, urns and roofs. They dated from the late nineteenth century and contained the bones of the great mill barons and their families. In *The Waste Land* T. S. Eliot wrote of the 'silk hat on a Bradford millionaire'. Now the mills and the millionaires had nearly disappeared. In the cemetery there were some white youths on a Youth Opportunity Scheme, hacking unenthusiastically at the weeds, clearing a path. This was the only work that could be found for them, doing up the old cemetery.

I was staying in a house near the cemetery. The houses were of a good size, well-built with three bedrooms and lofts. Their

front doors were open and the street was full of kids running in and out. Women constantly crossed the street and stood on each others' doorsteps, talking. An old man with a stick walked along slowly. He stopped to pat a child who was crying so much I thought she would explode. He carried on patting her head, and she carried on crying, until finally he decided to enter the house and fetched the child's young sister.

The houses were overcrowded – if you looked inside you would usually see five or six adults sitting in the front room – and there wasn't much furniture: often the linoleum on the floor was torn and curling, and a bare lightbulb hung from the ceiling. The wallpaper was peeling from the walls.

Each house had a concrete yard at the back, where women and young female children were always hanging out the washing: the cleaning of clothes never appeared to stop. There was one man – his house was especially run-down – who had recently acquired a new car. He walked round and round it; he was proud of his car, and occasionally caressed it.

It was everything I imagined a Bradford working-class community would be like, except that there was one difference. Everyone I'd seen since I arrived was Pakistani. I had yet to see a white face.

The women covered their heads. And while the older ones wore jumpers and overcoats, underneath they, like the young girls, wore *salwar kamiz*, the Pakistani long tops over baggy trousers. If I ignored the dark Victorian buildings around me, I could imagine that everyone was back in their village in Pakistan. . . .

That evening, Jane – the friend I was staying with – and I decided to go out. We walked back down the hill and into the centre of town. It looked like many other town centres in Britain. The subways under the roundabouts stank of urine; graffiti defaced them and lakes of rain-water gathered at the bottom of the stairs. There was a massive shopping centre with unnatural lighting; some kids were rollerskating through it, pursued by three pink-faced security guards in paramilitary outfits. The shops were also the same: Rymans, Smiths, Dixons, the National Westminister Bank. I hadn't become accustomed to Bradford and found myself making simple comparisons with London. The clothes people wore were shabby and old; they looked as if they'd been bought in jumble sales or second-hand shops. And their faces had an unhealthy aspect: some were malnourished.

As we crossed the city, I could see that some parts looked old-fashioned. They reminded me of my English grandfather and the Britain of my childhood: pigeon-keeping, greyhound racing, roast beef eating and pianos in pubs. Outside the centre, there were shops you'd rarely see in London now: drapers, ironmongers, fish and chip shops that still used newspaper wrappers, barber's shops with photographs in the window of men with Everly Brothers haircuts. And here, among all this, I also saw the Islamic Library and the Ambala Sweet Centre where you could buy spices: dhaniya, haldi, garam masala, and dhal and ladies' fingers. There were Asian video shops where you could buy tapes of the songs of Master Sajjad, Nayyara, Alamgir, Nazeen and M. Ali Shahaiky.

Jane and I went to a bar. It was a cross between a pub and a night-club. At the entrance the bouncer laid his hands on my shoulders and told me I could not go in.

'Why not?' I asked.

'You're not wearing any trousers.'

I looked down at my legs in astonishment.

'Are you sure?' I asked.

'No trousers,' he said, 'no entry.'

Jeans, it seems, were not acceptable.

We walked on to another place. This time we got in. It too was very smart and entirely white. The young men had dressed up in open-necked shirts, Top Shop grey slacks and Ravel loafers. They stood around quietly in groups. The young women had also gone to a lot of trouble: some of them looked like models, in their extravagant dresses and high heels. But the women and the men were not talking to each other. We had a drink and left. Jane said she wanted me to see a working men's club.

The working men's club turned out to be near an estate, populated, like most Bradford estates, mostly by whites. The Asians tended to own their homes. They had difficulty acquiring council houses or flats, and were harassed and abused when they moved on to white estates.

The estate was scruffy: some of the flats were boarded up,

rubbish blew about; the balconies looked as if they were about to crash off the side of the building. The club itself was in a large modern building. We weren't members of course, but the man on the door agreed to let us in.

There were three large rooms. One was like a pub; another was a snooker room. In the largest room at least 150 people sat around tables in families. At one end was a stage. A white man in evening dress was banging furiously at a drum-kit. Another played the organ. The noise was unbearable.

At the bar, it was mostly elderly men. They sat beside each other. But they didn't talk. They had drawn, pale faces and thin, narrow bodies that expanded dramatically at the stomach and then disappeared into the massive jutting band of their trousers. They had little legs. They wore suits, the men. They had dressed up for the evening.

Here there were no Asians either, and I wanted to go to an Asian bar, but it was getting late and the bars were closing, at ten-thirty as they do outside London. We got a taxi and drove across town. The streets got rougher and rougher.

[. . .]

When I was in my teens, in the mid-sixties, there was much talk of the 'problems' that kids of my colour and generation faced in Britain because of our racial mix or because our parents were immigrants. We didn't know where we belonged, it was said; we were neither fish nor fowl. I remember reading that kind of thing in the newspaper. We were frequently referred to as 'second-generation immigrants' just so there was no mistake about our not really belonging in Britain. We were 'Britain's children without a home'. The phrase 'caught between two cultures' was a favourite. It was a little too triumphant for me. Anyway, this view was wrong. It has been easier for us than for our parents. For them Britain really had been a strange land and it must have been hard to feel part of a society if you had spent a good deal of your life elsewhere and intended to return: most immigrants from the Indian subcontinent came to Britain to make money and then go home. Most of the Pakistanis in Bradford had come from one specific district, Mirpur, because that was where the Bradford mill-owners happened to look for cheap labour twenty-five years ago. And many, once here, stayed for good; it was not possible to go back. Yet when they got older the immigrants found they hadn't really made a place for themselves in Britain. They missed the old country. They'd always thought of Britain as a kind of long stop-over rather than the final resting place it would turn out to be.

But for me and the others of my generation born here, Britain was always where we belonged, even when we were told – often in terms of racial abuse – that this was not so. Far from being a conflict of cultures, our lives seemed to synthesize disparate elements: the pub, the mosque, two or three languages, rock 'n' roll, Indian films. Our extended family and our British individuality co-mingled.

[. . .]

There is a word you hear in Bradford all the time, in pubs, shops, discos, schools and on the streets. The word is 'culture'. It is a word often used by the New Right, who frequently cite T. S. Eliot: that culture is a whole way of life, manifesting itself in the individual, in the group and in the society. It is everything we do and the particular way in which we do it. For Eliot culture 'includes all the characteristic activities of the people: Derby Day, Henley regatta, Cowes, the Twelfth of August, a cup final, the dog races, the pin-table, Wensleydale cheese, boiled cabbage cut into sections, beetroot in vinegar, nineteenth-century gothic churches and the music of Elgar.'

If one were compiling such a list today there would have to be numerous additions to the characteristic activities of the British people. They would include: yoga exercises, going to Indian restaurants, the music of Bob Marley, the novels of Salman Rushdie, Zen Buddhism, the Hare Krishna Temple, as well as the films of Sylvester Stallone, therapy, hamburgers, visits to gay bars, the dole office and the taking of drugs.

Merely by putting these two, rather arbitrary, lists side by side, it is possible to see the kinds of changes that have occurred in Britain since the end of the war. It is the first list, Eliot's list, that represents the New Right's vision of England. And for them unity can only be maintained by opposing those seen to be outside the culture. In an Oxbridge common-room, there is order, tradition, a settled way of doing things. Outside there is chaos: there are the barbarians and philistines.

Among all the talk of unity on the New Right, there is no sense of the vast differences in attitude, life-style and belief, or in class, race and sexual preference, that *already* exist in British society: the differences between those in work and those out of it; between those who have families and those who don't; and, importantly, between those who live in the North and those in the South. Sometimes, especially in the poor white areas of Bradford where there is so much squalor, poverty and manifest desperation, I could have been in another country. This was not anything like the south of England.

And of course from the New Right's talk of unity, we get no sense of the racism all black people face in Britain: the violence, abuse and discrimination in jobs, housing, policing and political life. In 1985 in Bradford there were 111 recorded incidents of racist attacks on Asians, and in the first three months of 1986 there were seventy-nine.

But how cold they are, these words: 'in the first three months of 1986 there were seventy-nine.' They describe an Asian man being slashed in a pub by a white gang. Or they describe a Friday evening last April when a taxi company known to employ Asian drivers received a 'block booking' for six cabs to collect passengers at the Jack and Jill Nightclub. Mohammed Saeed was the first to arrive. He remembers nothing from then on until he woke seven hours later in the intensive care ward of the hospital. This is because when he arrived, his windscreen and side window were smashed and he drove into a wall. And because he was then dragged from the car, kicked and beaten on the head with iron bars, and left on the pavement unconscious. He was left there because by then the second taxi had arrived, but Mohammed Suleiman, seeing what lay ahead, reversed his car at high speed: but not before the twenty or thirty whites rushing towards him had succeeded in smashing his windows with chair legs and bats. His radio call, warning the other drivers, was received too late by Javed Iqbal. 'I was,' he told the *Guardian* later, 'bedridden for nearly a fortnight and I've still got double vision. I can't go out on my own.'

*Hanif Kureishi*

# Group discussion

**What kind of view of British society does the reader get from this examination of Bradford?**

Before you try to answer this question, work on the following tasks which will help you to organise your thoughts.

(a) The passage falls into three clearly defined sections. With a partner, work through each section making notes on what Kureishi has to say about the following topics:

| | |
|---|---|
| class | culture |
| race | poverty and wealth |
| the position of women | |

(b) As you go through the piece, give each section a title that identifies its most important aspect.

## Suggestions for writing

1 The way that you respond to this article depends very much on the sort of person you are; your sex, race, political views and where you live. You might, for instance, live in Bradford, in which case your attitude will be very different from someone who lives in, say, the Scottish Highlands. However, in his introduction, Hanif Kureishi claims that Bradford tells us something about the state of Britain. Do you feel that it gives an accurate picture?

Using your notes from the task above, write about Kureishi's view of the country and relate it to your own experience of growing up in Britain in the 1980s and 1990s.

2 In the final section of this article, Kureishi gives two lists of what constitutes culture. The first is by T. S. Eliot, the second is Kureishi's modern version. What would your list be? Remember that it must include all the characteristic activities of people of your age. When you have chosen your list, use it as the basis for a piece of writing in which you examine the importance of each activity to your generation.

# A different view of Bradford

Here is another description of Bradford.

For the visitor, Bradford has much on offer. As an introduction, discover its history and industrial heritage by following the well-planned City Trail. Track down reminders of famous Bradfordians, among them, author J. B. Priestley, composer

Frederick Delius and painter David Hockney. Spend time in the city's museums and galleries which include the National Museum of Photography, Film and Television – Britain's newest and most exciting national museum. Its giant IMAX cinema, is an unforgettable experience. Browse round old streets or enjoy the bustle of the Kirkgate Arndale Centre. Hunt for textile bargains in the millshops and for bygones in the flea market. Sample some of the country's most-vaunted pies, fish 'n' chips and curries, and taste the classic roast beef and Yorkshire pudding on its home ground. Take in a symphony concert at St George's Hall or a pantomime at the Alhambra.

## Group discussion

- Where do you think this description comes from?
- When you have decided, write a short paragraph explaining the reasons for your decision.
- Now read the whole piece.

# BRADFORD – A SURPRISING PLACE

Bradford, on the fringe of the Yorkshire Dales, had uncertain beginnings: a Roman road, a Saxon chapel . . . yet, in the 1550s, a jostling market town which already 'standeth much by clothing'. In the ensuing centuries the woollen industry expanded and, subsequently benefiting from improved communications and the advent of steam power, brought Bradford increasing wealth. By the mid-1800s, the 'praty quik market toune' had risen to fame and fortune as the world's worsted capital. During its peak expansion period, 1810–50, the population grew from 16,000 to over 100,000 and the number of textile mills increased from 5 to 120; most of them produced fine worsted cloth, Bradford's speciality. The new-found prosperity of 'Worstedopolis' fostered magnificent building enterprises including the City Hall, a flamboyant Italianate flourish; Little Germany's palatial warehouses; the imposing Wool Exchange and even Undercliffe Cemetery with its extravagantly ornate memorials.

*Bingley Five Rise Locks*

Although wool is no longer dominant, Bradford continues as a major manufacturing and commercial centre, while modern development projects – such as restoring the Edwardian Alhambra to its full plush-and-gilt glory – rival the Victorians' in their ambition and vision.

For the visitor, Bradford has much on offer. As an introduction, discover its history and industrial heritage by following the well-planned City Trail. Track down reminders of famous Bradfordians, among them, author J. B. Priestley, composer Frederick Delius and painter David Hockney. Spend time in the city's museums and galleries which include the National Museum of Photography, Film and Television – Britain's newest and most exciting national museum. Its giant IMAX cinema, is an unforgettable experience. Browse round old streets or enjoy the bustle of the Kirkgate Arndale Centre. Hunt for textile bargains in the millshops and for bygones in the flea market. Sample some of the country's most-vaunted pies, fish 'n' chips and curries, and taste the classic roast beef and Yorkshire pudding on its home ground. Take in a symphony concert at St George's Hall or a pantomime at the Alhambra.

Beyond the city centre, Bradford's Metropolitan District encompasses open moors and wooded valleys. The various villages scattered across this hinterland have their own attractions: Haworth, home of the Brontës; Saltaire, workers' utopia; 'bah't 'at' Ilkley; canalside Bingley; moortop Queensbury and Oxenhope with its annual strawrace. Other traditional activities, linking past and present, include Morris dancing, brass bands, clog dancing and handbell ringing – all enjoyed throughout the region.

*Silsdon, near Keighley*

Bradford makes an ideal base for exploring the adjacent countryside. Reaching the city in the first place, with its comprehensive road, rail and air links, is equally effortless. And once there you will surely agree that Bradford is 'a surprising place'.

*English Tourist Board*

## Group discussion (cont.)

- Is this what you expected?

- As you can see, this extract gives a very different picture of the city from the way it was described by Hanif Kureishi. Why do you think this is?

- What are the main differences between this description of Bradford and Kureishi's? Discuss this within your group and make a list of what you see as the most important differences.

- To give you a clearer understanding of the nature of the English Tourist Board description, read through the leaflet with a partner and make a list of twenty 'Key Words'. These should be words that, in your opinion, give the leaflet its persuasive tone. Many of these will be adjectives, but be on the lookout for nouns and verbs too. When you have finished, compare your words with those of other groups. Are there certain words that all the groups have chosen?

- Now discuss these questions:

  (a) What sort of person does the English Tourist Board (ETB) intend to read its leaflet?

  (b) How does this intention affect the content, layout, tone, length and vocabulary of the leaflet?

# Comparing the two views of Bradford

## Group discussion

- Read the leaflet again and discuss the following statements. Which statements do you agree with? Which do you disagree with?

  (a) Kureishi's picture of Bradford is truthful.

  (b) The ETB is only interested in Bradford's past.

  (c) The people of Bradford will benefit from the ETB leaflet.

  (d) Kureishi set out to look for problems and so was bound to find them.

  (e) One of the extracts could be accused of racism.

  (f) Both extracts could be accused of racism.

  (g) The ETB presents a true picture of Bradford.

  (h) Both extracts are educational.

  When you have finished your discussion, compare your decisions with those of other groups.

• In each case, the publisher and possibly the writer have spent a great deal of time choosing photographs that will enhance the writing; adding to its power. Compare the photographs used to illustrate the two extracts. What do they tell you about the writer's intentions? How do they reflect the content of the writing?

## Suggestion for writing

Write a comparison of these two views of Bradford. In your essay you should comment on the following:

(a) the intentions of the writers

(b) the selection of the material

(c) the use of photographs

(d) the writers' style, tone and vocabulary

## Suggestions for extended work

Both the extracts you have just read can be used as models for your own writing.

**Kureishi's methods**

*Hanif Kureishi sets out to discover the truth about a city.*

*He observes closely and sets down what he sees.*

*He conducts interviews and transcribes them.*

*He draws conclusion from what he sees and hears.*

You could use Kureishi's methods to produce an interesting and unusual piece of coursework. You need not travel to a distant city, there are many fruitful areas for investigation close to home. Here are some examples.

I Investigate an area of school life. There are many issues on which teachers, parents, ancillary staff and pupils will have widely varying views. You could take a look at:

(a) The way options are chosen in the third year of school.

(b) Bullying.

  (c)  Whether boys and girls have equal educational opportunities.

  (d)  The advantages and disadvantages of setting or streaming pupils according to ability.

**2** Your own home town or village could be investigated. Have there been any major changes recently (road schemes, housing or industrial development, for instance)? How do people feel about them? You may be able to interview representatives from the local council or the developers.

Both these suggestions involve a great deal of thoughtful planning. This kind of work is fascinating and enormously satisfying when completed, but don't be tempted to go it alone. Even a professional like Hanif Kureishi had help with his research, so work with a partner or in a small group. You will need to make each member of the group responsible for one aspect of the article. Whatever subject you choose, your investigation should follow this plan:

  **i** An introduction explaining why you have chosen your subject and what you hope to discover.

 **ii** A description of the place.

**iii** A selection of interviews.

 **iv** Conclusions. These might come in your final section or you could put them at the end of each interview. On the other hand, you may feel that there are no realistic conclusions. In this case just let your interviews speak for themselves.

For this kind of work you will need a notepad and preferably a small portable tape-recorder. Remember that your own impressions are as important as the words of people interviewed and that your readers may not know the places that you write about so make sure you describe them effectively.

*Note*: Always be aware that your questions could raise some difficult issues so when you are interviewing, be as polite and diplomatic as possible.

### The ETB's methods
You could use these methods to produce a piece of coursework. Here are some suggestions:

**1** Design a leaflet to promote your school. There may already be one that is given to prospective parents. If so, study it and see if there are ways in which it could be improved. Remember, the selection of photographs and the layout of the leaflet are as important as the content. Perhaps you could aim your leaflet at the students themselves rather than their parents.

*The Tourist Board sets out to present the most attractive view possible in order to bring tourists to the city.*

*It selects only the information that will support this view.*

*It uses photographs that show aspects of the city that it thinks will attract tourists.*

**2** Design a leaflet to promote your area, town or village as a tourist attraction. Every part of the country has something to offer tourists. Even if you live in an inner city you will find that your borough is likely to have historical connections. However, some students who live in areas unlikely to attract tourists find that they have more fun if they parody this kind of leaflet. Whichever way you tackle the assignment, the methods used will be similar. Below is an example of a leaflet prepared by a student:

```
LONDON   BOROUGH   OF

V I S I T O R S     I N F O R M A T I O N - S H E E T


    THE RESIDENTS SAY 'GET LOST' WITH
              OPEN ARMS



Welcome to                    ; here you
will find nothing that you ever wanted.
Our entire department sends their condo-
lences to anyone considering moving into
this area, just visiting or squatting.
(You will find the telephone number of
the lunatic asylum at the bottom of the
next page.)
```

Our most famous sights include the
'streets of no return', where you get
suffocated to death by Big Mac contain-
ers, old fridges and other ozone un-
friendly items.  (Our motto is ' NEVER
LET THE STREETS STAY CLEAN'.)  Also, not
to be missed, are the drunks of St Meths,
guaranteed to throw up all over you.
Lastly, we have the highest rate of
house-breaking and bag-snatching this
side of Tehran.

We have pride in providing plenty of nice
drugs, e.g. heroin, gear, spliffs, selling joints, tea-bags and rizzla to
anybody under 18, and giving absolutely
no dole money whatsoever.

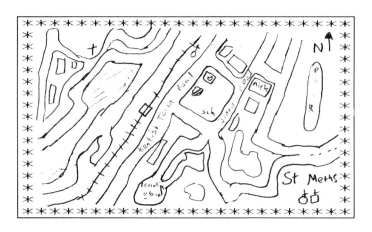

ENJOY YOUR STAY

Lunatic Asylum - 01 272 0021

# Investigation two

In the following article, Paul Hamann explains how, in 1987, he went about making a film of the last days in the life of Edward Earl Johnson, a convicted murderer.

# LAST DAYS ON DEATH ROW

**More than 70 people have been executed in the United States since the reinstatement of the death penalty in 1976; 1,900 others are awaiting their fate on America's 'Death Rows'. Edward Earl Johnson, a young black man from Mississippi, went to the gas chamber on 20 May this year. A BBC film crew spent the last 14 days of his life with him and, for them all, it was a shattering experience. This is Paul Hamann's story.**

> *Douglas Hurd, the Home Secretary, said at the recent Conservative Party conference that one of the reasons he was against the death penalty was because there was no redress for innocent men.*

United States opinion polls tell us Americans are in a punitive mood. In a country where there are nearly 450 murders every week, staying alive has become an endangered pursuit; people are frightened and angry and want retribution. When it comes to the death penalty, though, America keeps dubious company. Only one of its Nato allies, Turkey, is still executing people, though two or three other countries keep the penalty on their books. Iran and South Africa are the high legal killers and, although America is not in their league, it bucks the abolitionist trend with its numerous death sentences and the gathering speed of its executions. More disturbingly for a free democratic society, a convicted murderer in America is much more likely to be executed if he is poor, lives in the South and has killed a white person.

Talking in 1984 to Harold Washington, the black Mayor of Chicago, about a documentary on his fight to clean up his corrupt city, he implored me instead to make a film 'down South', looking at the fast-growing numbers on Death Rows there: 'It's a horrifying lottery of politics, money and race; where the crime was committed is more important than the nature of the crime itself.' Within weeks of my return to London from Chicago, the IRA – in one of its most horrifying acts – blew up the Grand Hotel in Brighton, where most of the British Cabinet were sleeping. In the following weeks, not surprisingly, there was much clamour in the Commons and our press to bring back the death penalty here. It seemed that this was certainly the time to take up Harold Washington's suggestion.

We approached most of the 37 States that have capital punishment, with a view to making the inside story through the eyes of the prison staff, inmates and lawyers during the final weeks of a death sentence. Gruesome though this would be, nearly everyone we spoke to who had been involved in an execution, said it had to be made then. 'Only then,' said one prison chaplain, 'can you show the full horror.' The Mississippi Department of Corrections (which still uses the gas chamber), after a stiff three-hour interview with me at a board meeting, eventually agreed that the film could be made, and invited me to meet their executioner: 64-year-old Berry Bruce.

Mr Bruce had held the job for many years and was paid $250 an execution. He seemed proud of the notoriety it gave him. He told me stories of being part of America's liberating forces at the Nazi death camps, and described with horror the gas chambers and the troughs of bodies. I asked him how he equated his obvious disgust at that with his last execution in 1983, when 'Jimmy Lee Gray' was reported by several witnesses to have had convulsions for eight minutes in the gas chamber and to have struck his head repeatedly on the pole behind him after Mr Bruce had thrown the death lever. Mr Bruce claimed to have had no feelings at all.

Since that chilling meeting in November 1984, there have been no executions in the State of Mississippi, and I was glad to put the place and the man out of my mind. But, last April, the phone rang at home one night. It was Don Cabana, Superintendent of the Mississippi State Penitentiary at Parchman, telling me the next execution would take place soon, in May. He said there was unlikely to be a stay, and that they'd sacked Berry Bruce and were looking for a new executioner.

I returned to Mississippi. Within an hour of being back in the prison, I began to feel rather numb. Many senior people there seemed to be looking forward to the execution. They showed me, with enthusiasm, their newly refurbished gas chamber. I

then met a 26-year-old black man from Walnut Grove, Mississippi – Edward Johnson.

Edward Johnson surprised me. He was quietly spoken, articulate and, unlike me that night, extremely relaxed. His story began eight years ago, in June 1979, when a white woman in Walnut Grove heard a knock at her door after midnight. When she answered, a black man assaulted but did not rape her. The local town marshal, Jake Trest, was passing and intervened. A struggle ensued and Mr Trest was shot and killed. Edward Johnson, then an 18-year-old high-school graduate, had a car breakdown that night in the vicinity of the crime. Because he made a phone call for repairs, his presence in the neighbourhood was quickly established.

Mr Johnson had been brought up by his grandparents. Both he and they were well known and liked in Walnut Grove. He had no criminal record. Yet the sheriff went at once to his home, picked him up and took him to the house of the woman who had been assaulted. Mr Johnson's grandmother insisted on accompanying them. Within hours of the assault and in the presence of his grandmother, the white woman said that Edward Johnson was not the man who had attacked her. Mr Johnson was immediately released.

Two days later, the sheriff again came to Johnson's home, saying he wanted to take Edward to Jackson (the Mississippi state capital) for a lie-detector test. According to Mr Johnson's later accounts, consistently repeated in court, he was not taken to Jackson but to the local woods, where the sheriff and other officers threatened him and his grandparents with violence. Under this pressure, said Mr Johnson, he confessed to the shooting of the town marshal.

At his first opportunity, he denied his confession and said he was scared: no one knew where he was; they threatened to shoot him and he finally signed the confession when violence was also threatened against his grandparents. After the confession had been made, the assaulted woman changed her story and (under duress, say Johnson's lawyers) identified Johnson as the man who had attacked her.

The disavowed confession and the woman's changed testimony were enough to convict Edward Johnson – who, it must be said, until he changed his lawyers a few weeks before his execution, appears to have been extremely badly and incompetently represented. His new lawyer, Clive Stafford Smith, an Englishman practising out of Atlanta, was horrified at how his case had been handled. Like many men on Death Row in the US, Johnson was poor and could not afford good legal representation.

> *'Who gets executed is still an arbitrary thing and depends on wealth, power and unusual circumstances. Most who are killed are poor and friendless.'*
>
> GOVERNOR OF FLORIDA

Throughout that long evening, telling me his story, Johnson calmly maintained his innocence – as he has done consistently throughout the last eight years. He said that he didn't believe they would or could execute him. He said that he had found God and therefore had nothing to fear.

*The US Supreme Court has publicly accepted a detailed statistical study of more than 2,000 murder cases in Georgia in the 1970s. The study found that a black man, convicted of killing a white (as was Edward Earl Johnson), was 4.3 times as likely to receive the death penalty as a white who had killed a black.*

We started filming on 7 May, 14 days before Mr Johnson's execution date. None of us on the production team, who spent those days with him, will ever forget them. Whatever one's feelings about the death penalty, there was no doubt in any of our minds that Mr Johnson's conviction was an extremely unsafe one.

That first evening he also told me that, after his car breakdown and at the time of the crime he was in a pool hall with a woman, a black woman. At the time, she went to the court house to volunteer her testimony, but was told by a white law-enforcement officer to go on home and mind her own business. None of Mr Johnson's lawyers attempted to find that woman and persuade a court to hear her during his eight-year fight to save his life. (Lawyer Clive Stafford Smith, tragically brought in very late on the case, located her the week after Mr Johnson was executed.)

During the first week's filming, I wasn't sure if Edward Johnson was guilty or not guilty. What became apparent, however, was that many of the prison officials and lawyers knew that in states outside 'The South' Edward Johnson would not be on Death Row and possibly not even convicted. As the tension mounted in Parchman Penitentiary and people got to know and trust my team and me, the prison doctor, chaplain, psychologist and many of the staff on Death Row all told us they believed Edward Johnson to be innocent. Increasingly, I began to find filming very difficult. I was getting to know Edward very well. We were playing chess every evening: he was the best player on the Row and thrashed me every time: 'Don't look so dejected, Paul. Remember I've had eight years to get my game into shape.' The process of filming became rather surreal: here we were filming someone's last days; most people around him thought he was innocent: he himself remained calm and adamant that they could not kill an innocent man. I wanted to say 'cut', and it would be all over.

The cameraman, Patrick O'Shea, and I began to wonder, as 20 May drew closer and the stress of Edward Johnson's predicament took hold of the whole penitentiary – staff and inmates alike – whether we should be filming at all, so intrusive we felt our presence to be. As ever, it was Edward who sharply admonished us for such feelings: 'I want, every man on this Death Row wants, this film made to show others what we have to go through. It's only just dawning on me that they want to kill me. They really want to kill me.' When he said that, there were three days to go. It was the first time he expressed a thought that his execution might actually take place.

That day, I met his mother for the first time, Betty Johnson. She now lives in New York and is a part-time policewoman there. She said: 'I know how they get confessions. I know how they got my son's.' While I talked to his mother, we could hear them testing the chamber outside. Edward Johnson had been hearing those unmistakable sounds for the last four weeks.

The Mississippi gas chamber looks a bit like an Apollo spacecraft, a small shiny steel capsule with a large, airtight door. Inside, a black metal chair with well-used leather straps. The Parchman execution team had tested the chamber several times with rabbits. The new executioner and his aides at one of these tests, in our presence, pretended there was a cyanide leak and collapsed. All the staff thought this was hilarious. This all took place outside Edward Johnson's cell. The windows were open; he and the rest of Death Row heard everything. There were two days to go.

I hope this doesn't sound melodramatic, but those last 48 hours were the worst of my life. His lawyer tried desperately in those last hours every final appeal possible. They were all turned down. His family were terribly brave. He was allowed to touch and hug them for the first time in eight years. The Death Row staff and head chaplain said on film they believed Edward Johnson to be innocent. Don Cabana, the efficient superintendent, became nervous and unsure.

With an hour to go, we heard that Governor Allain of Mississippi, a Catholic, had turned down the final plea for clemency. It was impossible to remain the impartial BBC onlooker, and I asked Don Cabana for permission to ring the governor. Governor Allain, of course, turned me down, too.

We filmed Edward in his cell in his last hour. Cabana, poor man, with his job to do, explained to him the final processes.

'Edward, in a few minutes two medical personnel will come in, they will tape two stethoscopes to your chest. They'll also tape two EKG terminals to you. They may have to shave a little hair off to do that. They'll put them on so that they can tell when your heart stops beating. OK?'

Cabana then asked the sound recordist, the cameraman and myself to leave. As tears welled in our eyes, Edward shouted 'Hey, don't do that. That's what they want you to do.' We all hugged him and left.

Just after midnight, they gassed Edward Earl Johnson to death. His lawyer later told me he showed signs of life for ten minutes after the cyanide entered the chamber.

*Paul Hamann wrote and produced* Fourteen Days in May *for BBC1.*

*from* The Listener, *12 November 1987*

## Group discussion

- This article tells the story of the making of a television documentary and deals with each stage of the story from the initial research to the execution. Split the article into sections and give each section a sub-heading. Make sure that your headings reflect the most important theme of each section.

- Some parts of the article have been printed in italics. What is the purpose of these paragraphs? How do they add to the effectiveness of the article?

- The article was obviously written to present the arguments against the death penalty. Imagine that you have been asked to produce a pamphlet to persuade MPs to vote against the re-introduction of capital punishment. You only have room for a short excerpt from this article. Which part would you choose and why?

## Suggestions for writing

1 This article is based on a television documentary called *Fourteen Days in May* which included filmed interviews with Johnson, Cabana and others but obviously there was no film of the events leading up to Johnson's imprisonment. It is usual in a programme of this kind to bring in scriptwriters and actors to produce a re-enactment of the events. Write a script for any of the events that Hamann describes

prior to Johnson's imprisonment. Here are the events you could dramatise:

(a)   The assault and shooting (this would contain little dialogue but would need a lot of careful description).

(b)   The sheriff picks up Johnson and his grandmother and takes them to the house of the assaulted woman.

(c)   The sheriff comes to the Johnson home and takes him away. He confesses under duress.

On page 23 you will find an example of a film script. Use it as a model for the way that you lay out your writing. You may like to include a narrator to tell the story or comment on the action. Your script should consist of these three elements:

(a)   dialogue spoken by the actors

(b)   narration of the events by the actor employed to narrate the documentary (optional)

(c)   descriptions of the images that the camera will show (including the way the actors should move and the way each scene should look). This will probably be the longest and most complicated part of your script.

You may find it clearer to write each of them in a different colour so as not to confuse your readers.

**2** How does Don Cabana feel about the execution? Write a speech for him in which he expresses his feelings and tries to make sense of his position. You could imagine him speaking directly to the camera or write it in the form of an interview with Paul Hamann.

**3** At the beginning of the article, Paul Hamann gives as one of his reasons for making the documentary the fact that many people in Britain are still calling for the return of the death penalty. Use this article as the first piece of evidence for an essay in which you discuss the moral and legal arguments for and against the reinstatement of capital punishment. You will need to research this subject in a variety of ways. Here are some suggestions:

(a)   Carry out a questionnaire amongst teachers and pupils in your school to find out how many of them support capital punishment. Remember that some people only want it reintroduced for certain crimes like terrorism or killing a policeman.

(b)   Research famous cases like Ruth Ellis, Timothy Evans, Craig and Bentley and The Guildford Four.

(c) Write to your local MP for his or her view.

Make sure your essay presents both sides of the debate before you give your own views.

# Investigation three

In 1978, Polly Toynbee spent a day with the training officer of an electrical engineering company. On this particular day he was interviewing six girls and, as you will see, Toynbee finds the girls' performances puzzling.

*Note*: Before GCSEs and Standard Grades were introduced there was a two-tier-exam system. A minority of academically able students took O Levels and the rest took the less demanding CSE exams.

# GIRLS' CAREERS

Opportunities being equal, the electrical engineering company was recruiting 35 persons to become craft and technical apprentices and 12 persons as secretarial and commerce trainees. But things being what they are, the first group were, of course, all boys, and the second group all girls.

The girls were being interviewed that day. Most had taken six or seven CSEs. They had all sat Morrisby tests beforehand, and their results, indicating something about their personalities and abilities, were sitting on the desk as they came into the room. There were over 60 applicants for the 12 jobs. I sat in on six of the interviews and they made depressing listening.

The first girl had a habit of saying 'Oh' after everything he said to her.

'You would go to college one day a week,' he was saying.

'Oh,' she said. 'Would I have to take exams?'

'Yes, at the end of the year.'

'Oh,' she said.

'Is there anything you would like to know about the work?'

'Oh, not really.'

He tried hard to strike up a conversation. 'What did you do in your special project in Home Economics?'

'Housing and that.'

'What did you find out about housing?'

'Oh, well, I went to estate agents and asked them.'

'What did you find out?'

'Rents are very expensive.'

He asked about her life outside school. 'What do you do with your time?' She was always slow to answer. 'Well, I go dancing, down the disco.'

'Have you got a boyfriend?'

'Not a regular one.'

'What else do you do?'

There was a long silence. 'I used to go the athletic club, but I gave it up.'

'Why?'

'I don't know really.'

'Do you do anything else?'

'I go to the pictures sometimes. I play records. I was in the Guides once.'

'What badges did you get?'

Another long silence before she said, 'Can't remember really.'

The training officer didn't feel he was getting far. No conversation was forthcoming and he had to drag these terse replies from her. 'Well,' he said, leaning across his desk, 'is there anything else you would like to know about the job?'

She started to shake her head, then asked, 'Would I be working with lots of girls?'

'Not always. Sometimes you would be with just one secretary.'

'Oh.'

When she had gone the officer said, 'She just has no drive.'

The next applicant had carefully curled dark hair. All the girls looked as if they had spent a long time with the blow-dryer and Carmen rollers. He started with her CSEs. She had taken seven. 'And I took one O Level,' she said. He looked up and asked what subject.

'Photography,' she said.

'Oh, that's most interesting. Why did you do that?' he asked, but his face fell a fraction when she said, 'Well, we had to do photography or art and I don't like art.'

'What do you do in photography?'

'Well, portraits, different angles, still life, and developing.'

'Do you ever do it on your own at weekends?'

She smiled. 'Not really,' she said.

'I see you did environmental studies. That sounds important. What is it?'

'Oh, pond life, you know. And pollution. It was boring.'

'Why did you do it?'

'Because it was the only subject I hadn't done before. I didn't know what it was really.'

'What's your favourite subject?'

'English.'

'Why is that?'

'I like essays. We had a nice exam.'

'What essay did you write?'

'Well, we had to write about a fantasy of a nice scene. I imagined I was on a beach in Spain with all nice music playing.'

'Well now, why do you want to work for us?' he asked in a friendly way.

'My dad says you're the only firm that trains secretaries. He works here, as a wireman.' He asked about her spare time. 'I used to do running, but not any more.'

'What do you do now?'

'Go down the discos mostly, I suppose,' she said.

Finally he asked if she had any questions. She took a list out of her handbag, and read out, 'What will my duties involve? What will my hours be? Will I have to go to college? Will I be entitled to join a social club? What will my salary for my age be?' He gave her the answers.

He asked: 'What are your ambitions? What sort of secretary do you want to be?'

'The top!' she said with a surprising burst of energy. 'Well, not really, I want to earn enough to drive about in my own car. Maybe I'd like to be a temp later on.' She probably couldn't have said anything more disastrous. The company would not be keen to train someone who was going to take off to become a temp.

The training officer had a short break before the next interview. He said that girl had been very typical. Not stupid, perhaps a bit above average ability, yet with no interests or enthusiasms. 'It's hard to tell the difference between these girls. Once they start work, over the next few years they begin to blossom out, but at 16, and at school they all seem to conform to exactly the same things. They dress the same, speak the same, and never seem interested in anything except records, boy friends and discos. In some ways I suppose they are a lot more mature than the boys. But the boys are far more varied as personalities when they come for interviews.'

I was curious about the Morrisby tests. The training officer explained that they covered a range of abilities, and involved such skills as writing the letter 's' forwards and backwards as many times as possible in ten seconds. It all sounded a bit like astrology or palmistry, but the officer said he had become convinced of their value. I asked if he could give me a portrait of the next candidate from the tests, before we met her.

'This girl is flexible, and she has greatly enhanced personal confidence. Her abilities are very great, stronger even than her personality. She's full of ideas too. She may come across with great confidence and a lot of ideas. On the other hand she may have found that her inner confidence and her many ideas have not earned her popularity, and she may have learned to modify that. She may not come across quite so confident. We may be on to a good thing.'

I imagined a bright-eyed, pert kind of girl. But in came a large ruddy-faced puddingy girl, with a look of embarrassment on her face. He said to her, 'Have you any questions you would like to ask? You've applied for our commercial scheme, and you've read the booklet. What would you like to know?'

She left a long pause before answering, 'Um, nothing really.'

'Why did you pick the commercial and not the secretarial?'

'Ah, well, I don't know really.'

'What was it about the commercial scheme you liked?'

She paused even longer and finally said, 'It appealed to me.'

He asked her why she had taken CSEs and not O levels. She looked quite baffled. 'I did English, maths, typing, computer studies, domestic science and biology. They just tell you what to do at school, though I did choose the typing.'

'Now, let's talk about you, and what makes you tick. What are your interests?'

'I go to a youth club, but it's not very interesting.'

'Do you like sport?'

'I like swimming sometimes.'

'Any other activities?'

'No, not really.'

Where was this self-confident girl of exceptional ability? He tried another tack. 'Are there any other subjects that you would have liked to do at school if you'd had the chance?'

'Not really.'

'Do you think you show your ability in exams?'

'I hope I do.'

'Do you have any hobbies, like collecting stamps?'

'Oh, no.'

He decided to be more direct with her. 'Look Janet, you appear to have a very great deal more ability than your CSEs suggest. Our tests show that you should be a high-flyer, an O level girl. Can you think of any reason why you haven't achieved more at school?' She looked a bit blank, and not much cheered by the news of her good test results. 'Why do you think that is?'

'I don't know. They didn't say I could have done O level. They just told me what to do.'

I don't think she believed that she had much potential – so much for all that 'inner confidence' in her personality tests.

When she had gone the training officer sat back in his chair and shook his head. 'That's a mystery,' he said. 'There must be something there. Maybe my assistant could get something out of her if he interviewed her. I couldn't get a spark. Her tests did say she was flexible. Maybe she's too flexible for her own good, and just bends under any suggestion. Perhaps she's had no stimulation. It's as if something has stopped her dead.'

The boys who come for interviews at 16 are all over the place, the training officer said. Some come in dirty jeans, others in ties. Some pretend to be keen on taking radios to pieces as they think it'll help with an electrical engineering apprenticeship. They have widely differing ideas about what the work involves and what it leads to. They ask questions. They may be hopelessly inarticulate, but they get across some feeling of their personality.

But what's happened to the girls? At this age it's as if someone has knocked them on the head. At school they have scarcely considered careers other than the traditional nursing, secretarial or hairdressing. Their apparent maturity has been bought at the high cost of absolute conformity. Among groups of girls of this age any oddness, any irregularity of dress, opinion, enthusiasm or behaviour casts you out of the group. The boys may have their own conventions, but they allow a far wider range of personality to be acceptable within the group.

The girls are so busy pretending to be little women that they haven't time for anything else. At 16 they can pass as adult, while boys are still boys. Because they can get themselves older boyfriends and lift themselves up into an adult world, they are prepared to sacrifice almost all of themselves in the effort. They mimic the outward signs of adulthood most successfully. Their lives are entirely given over to boys; going to discos to meet boys, pop music to fantasize about boys, make-up and hair styles to catch boys, preferably older boys. Interests outside these narrow fields are dangerous, might expose them to ridicule, or might link them perilously with school and child-hood.

It isn't until later when they are older and secure in adulthood, that they can afford to allow more of their own individual personalities to grow, but by then it's often too late. By then they are entrenched in traditional female occupations, limited and without chance of promotion. Janet was going to lose her chance of getting on to the commercial scheme, with its opportunities (albeit less than the boys') of promotion into management.

Instead she would probably get a job as an office junior somewhere, and be bored out of her mind by the time she was twenty. Later maybe she would be one of those clever, alert, slightly bitter working-class women, popping Valium, full of frustrated talent. Maybe it was just school that had blurred her sensibilities, but whatever it is that happens to children in school between 14 and 16, it happens worse to girls, with the result that they try for and get the worst jobs with the least opportunities.

Plenty of 16-year-olds are late developers who don't show their abilities until later at work. With luck the boys will have gone into a job, however lowly, that could lead somewhere. The girls will almost certainly be stuck in a job with no prospects.

*Polly Toynbee*
*from* The Way We Live Now, *ed. Bernard Levin*

## Group discussion

Polly Toynbee's article contains damning criticisms of British secondary education. She is talking about you and the effect that school has had on you. Are her criticisms fair?

Here are some questions to help you focus your discussion.

• Do boys and girls differ in the ways she describes?

• Why do the girls appear so dull?

• Would it have made a difference if the training officer had been a woman?

• This article was written in 1978. Have things changed since then?

• Does school treat boys differently from girls?

# Suggestions for writing

1 Some GCSE and Standard Grade students (particularly girls) have felt very angry after reading this article. Do girls of your age all 'dress the same, speak the same, and never seem interested in anything except records, boy friends and discos'? If you think that Polly Toynbee is mistaken in her analysis of what school does to girls, then you could write an essay in the form of a letter to her in which you disprove her arguments.

OR

You may be angry for a different reason – because you feel that Polly Toynbee is right. Girls *are* damaged by secondary school; they conform to the expectations portrayed in the media and reinforced by parents and friends. If you agree with the article, then write about how your own experiences endorse Toynbee's views.

2 How can a school help young women to achieve their potential? Write about your ideas for improving the opportunities for girls in your school. You could interview teachers, governors, parents and students to find out if they feel there is a problem and, if so, what they think should be done about it.

# *Investigation four*

As part of their book *Coping with a Nightmare*, the Institute for the Study of Drug Dependence undertook some research in which they interviewed the families of heroin addicts.

In this extract, the authors explore the reactions of people who have just discovered that a member of their family is using hard drugs.

# IT SEEMS LIKE THE SKY FALLS IN

## FINDING OUT ABOUT THE DRUG USE

**There is a great range and mixture of emotions that may be aroused when a person first realises that their child, husband, wife or other relative or close friend is using drugs. These emotions are likely to be very deeply felt. Mothers, in particular, react very strongly:**

[. . .]

'I think one reacts in two ways, either the family might be made tremendously angry, or they are made tremendously frightened and anxious, or a mixture of both. Some parents will be extremely aggressive about it.'

**Sometimes the emotions get directed inward rather than at the child or the drug dealers so that the parents blame themselves and worry that they have failed as parents. They feel that they are guilty in some way:**

[. . .]

'The chief reaction you feel is guilt, what I felt was "what can be the matter with me?", "what am I doing destroying my own children? The last thing I want to do and it's happening".'

[. . .]

'There's one side of you saying, well I don't know if I need to feel guilty, I did act for the best at the time, which is true. On the other hand, you look back and you can see things that perhaps you should have done. There has to be at some time a grey area where everything hadn't gone well. So you can't bear to see them suffering as much as they are. It's a sort of emotional blackmail, really grinding you down.'

**There may also be a feeling of deep loss, that all your child's promise and all your hopes for her have just come to this:**

'She had the talent, it was so sickening. She's got it all there, it's so sickening.'

[. . .]

'I just couldn't believe that this child whom I adored would actually have done that to us, I felt it was a personal betrayal really. How could she have done that to us?'

[. . .]

'Our doctor kept saying, keep calm and cool. Eventually I said, "It's all very well for you to say this, but it's impossible".'

[. . .]

## WHAT ABOUT THE FATHERS?

**A number of mothers feel that their husbands are more detached from the problems, and may be less caring:**

'I think a caring mum always cares, they hate to see their kids go wrong and hate to see their kids make a mess of their lives. I think some fathers find it difficult to handle the situation and they can seem to move away from it. Fathers are not as emotionally involved. A few families I've met, the fathers have found it difficult, they just cut off. They find they can't handle it, so they shut off and leave it to the mother. Or they write the kids off, they say, "leave home".'

**Perhaps also fathers see traditional assumptions about their roles as setting up barriers to their deeper involvement. One father who now regularly attends a parents group with his wife, was very conscious of this:**

'There is always the barrier between two things: the mother is always going to be protective towards the child and the father is always going to be the dominant one – teaching him to do the right things and making him live up to me, not to her, as it were. She is just there to look after him. That's just how it is –

now we are being sexist! – but that's the way it works and that's the way it is.'

[. . .]

'See, as a man, when it comes to the crunch in the house, the man makes the decisions most of the time. Alright, he may be manipulated by the women in the home, but I mean the man is looked towards when it comes to the crunch. The man has to make the decisions . . .'

[. . .]

'Perhaps – you've got a sort of reflection of masculine values on one side with the young man trying to prove himself, and the father perhaps responding in a way that is not understanding or not accepting this because it is not how the father would see masculine behaviour.'

**A different point of view is that fathers are simply less articulate about their feelings. As one father said:**

'I simply can't talk about it.'

[. . .]

**An experienced drugs counsellor was also aware of the different points of view:**

'Some fathers really do not want to know and would instantly reject the child once they hear about the drugs problem. For example, one father came in here just the other day and said, 'Well, if there's one rotten apple in the barrel you just throw it out don't you?' And this was before there had been any sort of trauma in the family. But if fathers can remain involved they do have something extra to offer. Fathers can sometimes be a bit more objective, perhaps a bit tougher. And they can add that other perspective to what the mothers are doing.'

[. . .]

**Of course, this may be a bit of a stereotype. Some fathers do get seriously involved in support groups. One father de-scribed how he felt bewildered and angry about the lack of male involvement in the groups that he attended:**

'You know, you see predominantly mothers – there must have been, in the rooms at Riverside, about 30 women and about 4

men and I was still so hostile or angry that the first question I
asked when I got up was, accusingly, 'Why are there so few
men?' as if it was their fault. And they just said, well that is just
the way it is, you know – it would be marvellous if there were
more men – and I thought I just don't understand what they're
talking about.'

**For this father, the most appropriate initial response was not
to sit around talking but to organise as a group of men and
literally fight the problem:**

'I went along to the few men there and said, "what are we doing
here? Let's leave the mothers to discuss this bloody problem,
we'll go out and get pick-axe handles and we'll find ourselves
some pushers and we will smash the bloody living daylights out
of them" – and thank God, everybody said "Dave, that just isn't
the way it is – just sit and listen and maybe you'll learn". And
there were flip little things that were said that were very, very
wise and profound, like "come back for six meetings and if
you're not satisfied we'll give you back your misery". And I
liked those sort of little quips and everything – so I thought, I'll
keep coming back.'

[. . .]

**Drugs problems may bring out underlying conflicts between a
husband and wife, even when the drug user is not living at
home:**

'How it didn't break us up I don't know. Now that Sam is away,
all I get from my husband is about Sam. He says that I never
told him about Sam. So still Sam is causing trouble even though
he's not here. But it was always me that was up in the night. I
always felt my husband didn't really care. You'd hear him
snoring away upstairs. He doesn't drink a lot but if it got bad
he'd go out for a pint and that was his relaxation. If I could do
that . . .'

**Sometimes the mother may feel her loyalties become very
divided:**

'Don't force me to make the choice whether I'm going to go
with her and help her, or stay with you, because I don't want to
make that choice.'

## BROTHERS AND SISTERS

**While so much attention is focused on the drug user, what is happening to any other children in the family?**

[. . .]

'Anna went very shy and she couldn't relate to her age group. I think it has affected her a tremendous amount and I'm sure people don't realise how much it affects the sisters, especially if there is only one.'

[. . .]

'I feel there can be a great deal of resentment that can start in the family because the addicted person is getting all the attention, for a long time. Everything is pivoting around that person or that person's sickness or addiction, and the others think, well we're behaving perfectly alright and they don't take the slightest notice. I don't come into it do I?'

*from* Coping with a Nightmare,
*Institute for the Study of Drug Dependence*

# Suggestions for writing

*Coping with a Nightmare* is intended to help addicts' families by telling them that they are not suffering alone. A book that enables worried people to read about how others have coped with similar problems is certainly a good idea. However, a book can only reach a few people. A TV play would reach many more.

Write a play or film script based on this chapter of the book in which a young heroin addict is discovered by her or his family. Use the information in the extract to make your play as realistic as possible in its portrayal of each member of the family. You may even take some of your dialogue from the interview extracts.

Before you start you will need to think carefully about the characters, because their personalities will dictate the way they react to the situation. You should also plan the various scenes of your play so that your audience will be able to see how each member of the family reacts.

Why not use the extract as the stimulus for some drama improvisation? Read through the quotes and pick one or two around which to build a character, then improvise a few scenes in the family home. This will enable you to explore your ideas before setting them down on to paper and it is a good way to establish believable characters.

# *Investigation five*

In 1963, just after the Playboy Club opened in New York, journalist Gloria Steinem decided to uncover the truth behind the glamorous facade of the Playboy empire. To do this she took a job as a Playboy Bunnygirl under the name of Marie Ochs.

Here is an entry from her diary which describes her first night's work as a bunnygirl. As you read it, remember that in 1963 what we now call the Women's Movement had not yet come into being and the notion of sexism was unknown.

# *I WAS A PLAYBOY BUNNY*

## *EVENING, TUESDAY 5TH*

The Bunny Room was chaotic. I was pushed and tugged and zipped into my electric-blue costume by the wardrobe mistress, but this time she allowed me to stuff my own bosom, and I was able to get away with only half a dry cleaner's bag. I added the tiny collar with clip-on bow tie and the starched cuffs with Playboy cuff links. My nameplate was centered in a ribbon rosette like those won in horse shows, and pinned just above my bare right hipbone. A major policy change, I was told, had just shifted name tags from left hip to right. The wardrobe mistress also gave me a Bunny jacket: it was a below-zero night, and I was to stand by the front door. The jacket turned out to be a brief shrug of imitation white fur that covered the shoulders but left the bosom carefully bare.

I went in to be inspected by Bunny Mother Sheralee. 'You look *sweet*,' she said, and advised that I keep any money I had with me in my costume. 'Two more girls have had things stolen from their lockers,' she said, and added that I should be sure and tell the lobby director the exact amount of money I had with me. 'Otherwise they may think you stole tips.' Table Bunnies, she explained, were allowed to keep any tips they might receive in cash (though the club did take up to 50 percent of all their charge tips), but hat-check Bunnies could keep no tips at all. Instead, they were paid a flat twelve dollars for eight hours. I told her that twelve dollars a day seemed a good deal less than the salary of two to three hundred dollars mentioned in the advertisement. 'Well, you won't work hat check all the time, sweetie,' she said. 'When you start working as a table Bunny, you'll see how it all averages out.'

I took a last look at myself in the mirror. A creature with three-quarter-inch eyelashes, blue satin ears, and an overflowing bosom looked back. I asked Sheralee if we had to stuff ourselves so much. 'Of course you do,' she said. 'Practically all the girls just stuff and stuff. That's the way Bunnies are supposed to look.'

The elevator opened on the mezzanine, and I made my professional debut in the Playboy Club. It was crowded, noisy, and very dark. A group of men with organizational name tags on their lapels stood nearby. 'Here's my Bunny honey now,' said one, and flung his arm around my shoulders as if we were fellow halfbacks leaving the field.

'Please, sir,' I said, and uttered the ritual sentence we had learned from the Bunny Father lecture: 'You are not allowed to touch the Bunnies.' His companions laughed and laughed. 'Boy oh boy, guess she told *you!*' said one, and tweaked my tail as I walked away.

The programmed phrases of the Bunny bible echoing in my mind, I climbed down the carpeted spiral stairs between the mezzanine ('Living Room, Piano Bar, buffet dinner now being served') and the lobby ('Check your coats; immediate seating in the Playmate Bar'), separated from the street by only a two-story sheet of glass. The alternative was a broad staircase in the back of the lobby, but that, too, could be seen from the street. All of us, customers and Bunnies alike, were a living window display. I reported to the lobby director. 'Hello, Bunny Marie,' he said. 'How's things?' I told him that I had fifteen dollars in my costume. 'I'll remember,' he said. I had a quick and humiliating vision of all the hat-check Bunnies lined up for bosom inspection.

There was a four-deep crowd of impatient men surrounding the Hat Check Room. The head hat-check Bunny, a little blond who had been imported from Chicago to straighten out the system, told me to take their tickets and call the numbers out to two 'hang boys' behind the counter. 'I'll give you my number if you give me yours,' said a balding man, and turned to the crowd for appreciation.

After an hour of helping men on with coats, scarves, and hats, the cocktail rush had subsided enough for the Chicago Bunny to show me how to pin numbers on coat lapels with straight pins or tuck them in hatbands. She gave me more ritual sentences. 'Thank you, sir, here is your ticket.' 'The information Bunny is downstairs to your right.' 'Sorry, we're unable to take ladies' coats.' (Only if the club was uncrowded, and the coats were not fur, was the Hat Check Room available to women.) She emphasized that I was to put all tips in a slotted box attached to the wall, smile gratefully, and not tell the customers that the tips went to the club. She moved to the other half of the check room ('The blue tickets are next door, sir') and sent a tall, heavy-set Swiss Bunny to take her place.

The two of us took care of a small stream of customers and talked a little. I settled down to my ever-present worry that someone I knew was going to come in, recognize me, and say 'Gloria!' If the rumor were true that one newspaper reporter and one news-magazine reporter had tried to become Bunnies and failed, the management must be alert to the possibility, and I had seen more than enough Sydney Greenstreet movies to worry about the club's reaction. If someone I knew did come in, I would just keep repeating 'There must be some mistake' and hope for the best.

Dinner traffic began, and soon there was a crowd of twenty men waiting. We worked quickly, but coats going in and out at the same time made for confusion. One customer was blundering about behind the counter in search of a lost hat, and two more were complaining loudly that they had been waiting ten minutes. 'The reason there's a line outside the Playboy Club,' said one, 'is because they're waiting for their coats.' A man in a blue silk suit reached out to pull my tail. I dodged and held a coat for a balding man with a row of ballpoint pens in his suit pocket. He put it on, but backward, so that his arms were around me. The hang boy yelled at him in a thick Spanish accent to 'Leave her alone,' and he told the hang boy to shut up. Three women in mink stoles stood waiting for their husbands. I could see them staring, not with envy, but coldly, as if measuring themselves against the Swiss Bunny and me. High up on the opposite wall, a camera stared down at all of us and transmitted the scene to screens imbedded in walls all over the club, including one screen over the sidewalk: '. . . the closed-circuit television camera that flashes your arrival throughout the

Club...' explained publicity folders. I was overcome by a
nightmare sensation of walking naked through crowds but the
only way back to my own clothes was the glass-encased stairway.
As men pressed forward with coats outstretched, I turned to
the hang boy for more tickets. 'Don't worry,' he said kindly,
'you get used to it.'

Business let up again. I asked the Swiss Bunny if she liked the
work. 'Not really,' she shrugged. 'I was an airline hostess for a
while, but once you've seen Hong Kong, you've seen it.' A man
asked for his coat. I turned around and found myself face-to-
face with two people whom I knew well, a television executive
and his wife. I looked down as I took his ticket and kept my
back turned while the boy found the coat, but I had to face him

again to deliver it. My television friend looked directly at me, gave me fifty cents, and walked away. Neither he nor his wife had recognized me. It was depressing to be a nonperson in a Bunny suit, but it was also a victory. To celebrate, I helped a slight, shy-looking man put on his long blue-and-white scarf, asked him if he and the scarf were from Yale. He looked startled, as if he had been recognized at a masquerade.

There were no clocks anywhere in the club. I asked the hang boy what time it was. 'One o'clock,' he said. I had been working for more than five hours with no break. My fingers were perforated and sore from pushing pins through cardboard, my arms ached from holding heavy coats, I was thoroughly chilled from the icy wind that blew each time a customer opened the door, and, atop my three-inch black satin heels, my feet were killing me. I walked over to ask the Chicago Bunny if I could take a break.

'Yes,' she said, 'a half-hour to eat, but no more.'

Down the hall from the Bunny Room was the employees' lounge, where our meal tickets entitled us to one free meal a day. I pulled a metal folding chair up to a long bare table, took my shoes off gingerly, and sat down next to two black men in gray work uniforms. They looked sympathetic as I massaged my swollen feet. One was young and quite handsome, the other middle-aged and graying at the temples: like all employees at the club, they seemed chosen, at least partly, for their appearance. The older one advised me about rolling bottles under my feet to relax them and getting arch supports for my shoes. I asked what they did. 'We're garbage men,' said the younger. 'It don't sound so good, but it's easier than your job.'

They told me I should eat something and gestured to the beef stew on their paper plates. 'Friday we get fish,' one said, 'but every other day is the same stew.'

'The same, except it gets worse,' said the other, and laughed. The older one told me he felt sorry for the Bunnies even though some of them enjoyed 'showing off their looks.' He advised me to be careful of my feet and not to try to work double shifts.

Back downstairs, I tried to categorize the customers as I checked their coats. With the exception of a few teenage couples, the majority seemed to be middle-aged businessmen.

Less than half had women with them, and the rest came in large all-male bunches that seemed entirely subsidized by expense accounts. I saw only four of the type pictured in club advertisements – the young, lean, nattily dressed Urban Man – and they were with slender, fashionable girls who looked rather appalled by our stuffed costumes and bright makeup. The least-confident wives of the businessmen didn't measure themselves against us, but seemed to assume that their husbands would be attracted to us and stood aside, looking timid and embarrassed. There were a few customers, a very few, either men or women (I counted ten), who looked at us not as objects but smiled and nodded as if we might be human beings.

The Swiss Bunny took a break and a hang boy began to give me a gentle lecture. I was foolish, he said, to put all that money in the box. The tips were cash. If we didn't take some, the man who counted it might. I told him I was afraid they would look in my costume and I didn't want to get fired. 'They only check you girls once in a while,' he said. 'Anyway, I'll make you a deal. You give me money. I meet you outside. We split it.' My feet ached, my fingers were sticky from dozens of sweaty hatbands, and my skin was gouged and sore from the bones of the costume. Even the half-hour dinner break had been on my own time, so the club was getting a full eight hours of work. I felt resentful enough to take him up on it. Still, it would hardly do to get fired for stealing. I told him that I was a new Bunny and too nervous to try it. 'You'll get over that,' he said. 'One Saturday night last week, this check room took in a thousand dollars in tips. And you know how much we get paid. You think about that.'

It was almost 4:00 am. Quitting time.

The lobby director came over to tell us that the customer count for the night was about two thousand. I said that sounded good. 'No,' he said. 'Good is four thousand.'

I went back to the Bunny Room, turned in my costume, and sat motionless, too tired to move. The stays had made vertical indentations around my rib cage and the zipper had left a welt over my spine. I complained about the costume's tightness to the Bunny who was sitting next to me, also motionless. 'Yeah,' she said, 'a lot of girls say their legs get numb from the knee up. I think it presses on a nerve or something.'

The street was deserted, but a taxi waited outside by the employees' exit. The driver held a dollar bill out the window. 'I got four more of these,' he said. 'Is that enough?' I kept on walking. 'What'sa matter?' he said, irritated. 'You work in there, don't you?'

The streets were brightly lit and sparkling with frost. As I walked the last block to my apartment, I passed a gray English car with the motor running. A woman was sitting in the driver's seat, smoking a cigarette and watching the street. Her hair was bright blond and her coat bright red. She looked at me and smiled. I smiled back. She looked available – and she was. Of the two of us, she seemed the more honest.

*from* Outrageous Acts and Everyday Rebellions *by Gloria Steinem*

## Group discussion

Gloria Steinem later went on to become an influential feminist. In 1983 when this diary was republished, she added a postscript. In it she says that she later realised that 'all women are Bunnies'. What do you think she meant by this statement? To help you with your discussion, here are some questions:

(a)  How is she made to dress?

(b)  Is she paid well?

(c)  How is she treated by the male customers?

(d)  How is she treated by the female customers?

(e)  In what way is she on display?

(f)  In what way is she invisible?

(g)  Why aren't the women called 'Rabbitwomen'?

## Suggestions for writing

1  How do you think the Playboy organisation and real bunnygirls would have reacted if they had found out 'Marie Och's' real purpose? Write a version of what might have happened. You could do it as an entry in Gloria Steinem's diary or as an objective account. Your writing should include:

  (a)  an interview with the 'Bunny Mother' (Gloria's immediate boss) in which Gloria Steinem explains why she became a Bunnygirl and what she has learned from the experience;

(b) a conversation with a real Bunnygirl in which Gloria Steinem reveals the truth and explains her purposes.

**2** Use a discussion of Gloria Steinem's statement that 'all women are Bunnies' as the basis for an essay in which you compare Steinem's experiences as a Bunnygirl with the experiences of women in general. Is a Bunnygirl merely an extreme version of the image all women are supposed to adopt? In your essay you should include your views on the following issues:

(a) employment opportunities for women

(b) the representation of women in advertising

(c) the image of women in the media

(d) women's fashions (are they designed just to please men?)

(e) how you think the role of women will change in the future.

# *Extensions*

**1** If you enjoy reading investigations then try these:

*Down and Out in Paris and London* by George Orwell (Penguin) – Orwell decides to find out what it is like to be homeless in these two great cities.

*The Crack* by Sally Bellfrage (Grafton) – Bellfrage goes to Belfast to find out about the 'troubles' at first hand.

**2** It is obviously very difficult to work undercover like Gloria Steinem but that is not the only way a journalist can expose exploitation. She could, for instance, have written an article based on interviews with Bunnygirls.

You may have experienced exploitation yourself or know of examples of the exploitation of others. Some people, for example, have said that young people are often exploited by unscrupulous employers who pay them very little for a great deal of hard work.

Is there some practice that you think ought to be exposed? If so, undertake your own investigation and write it up in the form of an article. You never know, it might change things!

# 6 DEBATES

In our complex society we are surrounded by issues that seem to be constantly under discussion; the rights of animals, for instance, or whether we should allow experimentation on human embryos.

These important debates centre on questions of morality, to which there can be no simple 'right' answers. Often these questions are posed as a result of advances in modern technology or medicine and occasionally they are so scientifically difficult that we feel they must be left to the experts. However, there are many issues upon which we can enter the debate on equal terms with the experts, our informed opinion being as valid as any scientist's. This unit deals with some of these issues and contains the writing of both specialists and ordinary informed people.

The unit begins with a discussion of the value of zoos which is arranged like a formal debate. The motion is that 'Zoos have no function in the twentieth century'; the speakers for and against are represented by two newspaper articles.

# *Zoos – are they educational or barbaric?*

Most of us have visited a zoo during our childhood and been delighted by the sight of exotic animals at close quarters. Some people, however, react in a very different way. To them, the sight of a caged animal is a horrific reminder of mankind's continuing abuse of the natural world.

Recently, the *Independent* newspaper commissioned two experts to write articles expressing their opposing views on the value of zoos.

## *Group discussion*

Before you read the articles, discuss these statements taken from them. Decide whether you think each statement would be used *for* zoos or *against* them and arrange them in two columns accordingly.

(a) Three and a half years ago at London Zoo, a female African elephant was 'put to sleep' with a lethal drug overdose.

(b) In the past, collections of animals were assembled largely to entertain the public or to satisfy a private whim.

(c) For many people, especially living in towns, this is the closest they will come to seeing wild animals.

(d) Italy has [...] gone as far as to call for referendums on whether zoos should be allowed to exist.

(e) Veterinary information obtained in captivity on the capture, handling and transport of animals has proved vital to the successful relocation of wild animals.

(f) The number of species 'helped' by zoos amounted to a handful in 150 years.

Compare your arrangement of the statements with those of other groups. Make sure that you can defend your decisions.

Now read both articles carefully.

# NOT PRISONS FOR ANIMALS BUT RESERVOIRS OF SPECIES

*DAVID JONES ARGUES THAT AN IMPORTANT NEW ROLE HAS EVOLVED FOR ZOOS*

Zoos are under a lot of pressure these days to justify their existence. In the past, collections of animals were assembled largely to entertain the public or to satisfy a private whim. There was often little understanding of the animal's biological or behavioural needs, and even less perception of a responsibility to justify the collection in terms of science, conservation or popular education. For responsible zoos, this has changed dramatically.

The process of change has been stimulated by a variety of influences. The first was the recognition that the world's wildlife resources were finite; more to the point, they were declining. More and more legislation protecting species, greater expense in obtaining animals, and stricter health regulations governing the import of exotics, all generated a re-evaluation of the need to obtain animals from the wild.

Simultaneously, the science of exotic animal care developed the veterinary techniques and management expertise necessary to create captive environments where populations of animals flourished and reproduced successfully. To ensure that these populations were maintained and, where necessary, increased, zoos established co-operative arrangements amongst themselves to facilitate the exchange of animals and information. Stud books, often computerised, are maintained to ensure that

the captive population is kept genetically healthy and to avoid inbreeding. The result of these measures has been the development, over the last 15 years, of a new role for zoos, in which they contribute directly to the conservation of species in the wild and, where 'the wild' no longer exists, preserve species from complete extinction.

Ultimately, the conservation of animals and plants in the wild depends upon recognition of their financial, scientific or cultural importance. Such recognition takes time to develop. By acting as a reservoir for species, zoos can act as a safety device in case the species become extinct in nature. Zoos can also provide the animals necessary to reintroduce species extinct in the wild once the threats to their survival have been controlled.

For example, in 1982 the government of Oman reintroduced the Arabian oryx to the wild using animals bred for several generations entirely in zoos. In the process, local consciousness of the need for conservation was enormously heightened and a unique centre for desert research was developed. The examples so far of successful reintroduction are few, but this is because the technology required – and the need – has only developed in the last 20 years. Yet this is an area of immense potential.

Species are becoming extinct all the time. Only last week it was announced that the Partula snail had disappeared from the single Pacific island where it occurred. Zoos now represent the only hope for this tiny creature. Plans to reintroduce scimitar-horned oryx, Addax and Dama gazelles into North Africa are well under way. Ten oryx have already been released into Tunisia and there are also programmes to reintroduce Przewalski horses and Bali mynahs, to name but two of at least 100 potential candidates.

A second important function of any good zoo must be the education of the visitor. Regardless of the scientific expertise of the individual, he or she can expect to learn something every time he walks through the zoo gate. Catering to the intellectual demands of a spectrum of educational and age groups, so that they learn something – and appreciate it – is not easy. At the Zoological Society of London (ZSL) we maintain a large education department and graphics unit specifically to inform our visitors about the animals – where they come from, what they like to eat, how many babies they have, etc.

For many people, especially those living in towns, this is the closest they will come to seeing wild animals. Even with the high quality of the current wildlife films, there is no replacement for seeing the real thing. One must appreciate that for many people an animal simply isn't real if they only see it on a television screen. For those for whom a trip to Africa or South America to see the animal (if they are lucky) in the wild is impossible, zoos provide an opportunity to make the emotional and rational commitment essential to the future of conservation.

Finally, it should be appreciated that zoos provide a unique opportunity for research, the results of which may be crucial to the survival of species. Veterinary information obtained in captivity on the capture, handling and transport of animals has proved vital to the successful relocation of wild animals.

Reproductive information, again obtained in captivity, has been extremely useful to field studies. For example, analysis at ZSL of rhino urine makes it possible to pinpoint exactly when the female is in oestrus and when she becomes pregnant – significant information for a project in Kenya on the biology of rhinos. Zoos provide a wealth of information in other ways too. Data on the analysis of elephant milk, for example, allows us to provide the correct dietary substitute for orphaned elephants in Kenya. Zoo personnel are involved in field projects all over the world, either by making their specialised knowledge available or by themselves participating directly in these projects.

Apart from the debate over whether zoos perform a valuable role in society, they are often attacked on animal welfare grounds – that they are little more than prisons, exploiting their inhabitants for commercial purposes. British zoos themselves have recognised the need to improve standards, and both the Zoo Licensing Act (the only specific legislation of its kind in

Europe) and the British Federation of Zoos have established standards for keeping animals which will have to be achieved in the near future.

The word 'zoo' is loosely used to describe a variety of operations, many of which are nothing more than roadside menageries still aimed solely at providing popular entertainment and making a commercial profit for their owners. Such enterprises are often deservedly criticised, and some have closed with the coming of the Zoo Licensing Act. Unfortunately there is a tendency to tar all zoos with the same brush, regardless of fundamental differences in their philosophy, the quality of care given to their animals, and their contribution to science and conservation.

Nobody is arguing that zoos are perfect or that they are a substitute for the wild. But it is important to place them – the responsible, good zoos – in the overall context of conservation, and to recognise that they and the staff they support have a valuable role to play in the future.

*David Jones is Director of Zoos for the Zoological Society of London, which administers London and Whipsnade zoos.*

*from the* Independent, *August 1989*

# ANIMALS ARE BORN FREE BUT EVERYWHERE THEY ARE BEHIND BARS

*WILL TRAVERS ARGUES THAT ZOOS HAVE OUTLIVED THEIR USEFULNESS*

Three and a half years ago at London Zoo, a female African elephant was 'put to sleep' with a lethal drug overdose. Nothing so extraordinary in that; all over the world, zoo animals are destroyed on a regular basis because they are old or sick – or 'surplus to requirements'.

But Pole Pole was different. Once a film star with my parents, Bill Travers and Virginia McKenna, in *An Elephant Called Slowly*, her short movie career ended when she was shipped as a gift to London Zoo – one of the premier zoological collections in the world.

Twelve years later, we received a disturbing letter. Pole Pole was about to be destroyed. Our investigations revealed that she had been kept in solitary confinement at the zoo for almost two years and had become 'difficult to manage'. To be brief, the zoo rejected an offer to take Pole Pole to join a small elephant herd in an African game reserve, but decided she could go to the Zoological Society's elephant group at Whipsnade Zoo.

We were assured that she would not be put down unless it was 'the best thing for her'. In spite of the zoo's vast experience in moving animals, something went wrong. An injured foot, a septic infection – the lethal overdose was eventually prescribed.

This was the breaking point. Privately, my family had been critical of zoos and the concept of caging collections of animals for human 'enlightenment' and 'entertainment' since the making of the film *Born Free*. Now the public outcry at this needless death made it clear that thousands of people were as disturbed by the concept and reality of zoos as we were. The Zoo Check Trust was formed as our way of trying to seek a better deal for wildlife.

The latest plank in our campaign is a major EC-funded survey of European zoos, which we hope will have the effect of forcing a change in the law to improve animals' conditions.

Our intention, through Zoo Check, has been to put an end to such sights at zoos as the crazy antics of a bear as it sways from side to side or stands incessantly nodding its head to an imaginary beat; birds of prey unable to fly, only flap; tigers, solitary, nocturnal hunters, reduced to pacing the perimeter of a pauper's kingdom; giraffes lazily licking the leafless twigs of token trees. For humans, imprisonment is a punishment – no less so for animals.

Faced with such criticism, zoos felt compelled to re-state the justification for their existence. Top of the list was education. Without zoos, how would the thousands of children who cannot afford to visit the African game parks be able to see and smell a real live elephant?

But this was not the message we were getting from the children. Faced with the bleak sterility of the zoo, many children said they could 'feel' the misery, boredom and suffering. Surely, the animals' 'right' to a life of self-determination and freedom far outweighed the human 'right' to observe them in captivity. In any case, with the proliferation of superb wildlife film, which revealed wild animals in their natural environment, what was the educational value of seeing a bear wandering ceaselessly round a slab of blue-rinsed concrete?

Very well, critics pointed out, zoos were vital for conservation. Had not they already saved species like the Arabian oryx and Père David's deer from extinction? But the closer we looked at the conservation argument, the less convincing it became. The number of species 'helped' by zoos amounted to a handful in 150 years.

Besides, conservation by zoos seemed very expensive: £15m to save the Arabian oryx, £15m to try to save the Californian condor. Worldwide, zoos are spending in the region of £300m annually, an income generated from a mixture of gate receipts, state subsidy and private sponsorship. Money well spent? Schemes to conserve irreplaceable areas of rainforest, the richest, ecosystem in the world, are crying out for a few hundred thousand pounds. Somewhere, we humans have got our priorities sadly wrong.

Finally, zoos claimed to be centres of research. But research into what? Mainly, it transpired, on how best to look after wildlife – in captivity. Zoo Check, too, wanted to undertake research, but this time to see if it could be shown, beyond any reasonable doubt, that certain species were not candidates for captivity.

Our first survey, sponsored with Zoo Check money but undertaken independently, found that 60 per cent of polar bears in British zoos were mentally disturbed, and that their abnormal behaviour was induced by their captive environment. On the strength of these findings, a Zoo Check petition with 21,000 signatures called upon the National Federation of Zoos to make a public statement that, in future, no more bears would be kept in captivity. As yet, no such policy decision has been taken.

Zoo Check has now initiated two further surveys, one on great apes and the other on pachyderms (elephants, etc), to be conducted by independent biologist Ian Redmond. Sadly, though predictably, the Federation has decided not to co-operate with these studies.

It is significant that our forthcoming survey of European zoos, which will review living conditions, breeding records and mortality rates in all the zoos in the EC, has been substantially funded by the EC itself. Not in quite the same way that London Zoo receives a grant of around £2m a year from the British taxpayer, but £27,000 (to be matched pound for pound by money raised by Zoo Check) well spent. For if the British zoo establishment is slow to change and is happy simply to comply with the requirements of a rather weak Zoo licensing Act, the Europeans are in a more determined mood. Italy has even gone as far as to call for referendums on whether zoos should be allowed to exist.

The zoological collection is an 'endangered species'. Maybe it was once relevant, when the world was large, animals were 'dumb' and television was not invented. But now is the time for change. The more enlightened zoo people have seen it coming and are switching sides. Politicians are considering their position in the debate and calling for change; scientists and vets are keen to explore new ways of helping wildlife outside the zoo environment; philosophers are considering the argument in the same way as their predecessors did slavery; and the public,

increasingly concerned and better informed than ever, is carefully making up its mind.

The question is, can we knowingly support the suffering of animals in zoos, or do we act now to secure a future for wildlife in the wild?

*from the* Independent, *August 1989*

## Group discussion (cont.)

- Work in groups of three or four and read the articles together. Discuss the material as you read it.
- You may find that you all agree on the zoo debate.

  If that is the case, concentrate on the article that you disagree with and make sure that, between you, you can produce arguments that answer all the points made in the article. When you are satisfied, put together a group statement that expresses your views clearly and concisely (no more than half a side of A4).

- There may be a difference of opinion within your group

  If so, work out exactly where each of you stands on the issue and try to come up with a group statement that reflects these differences.

- Each group should read out its statement. What is the general feeling of the class?

Before you commit yourself to any writing, read the following extracts from articles by two established novelists, Angela Carter and Angus Wilson.

# AT THE ZOO

A small colony of monkeys inhabited a roomy cage full of greenery; all was not oppressively chic, but green and decent. As in a very good sanatorium, all was order and decency. A pair of baboons sat together on a bough like Darby and Joan. In an adjoining cage, a very nice black gibbon with a white beard did a few press-ups.

He swung to the front of his cage when he saw us and thrust both his long arms through the bars, opening and closing his black, wrinkled, distressingly humanoid hands but not quite as if he were begging for food, more as if beseeching us for something. And he must have known we would not give him food for there were notices everywhere: 'It is vehemently forbidden to feed the animals.' (When I was working at the zoo in Bristol once, I saw a man feed a little rhesus monkey with a ball-point pen.) No. It seemed as if he wanted to hold hands.

When nothing was forthcoming from us, no reciprocal gesture, he reached right out to the grass that grew outside his cage, pulled up a few stalks, all that he could reach, and munched them. So it *was* goodies he was after! But his bowl was full of lots of delicious looking fruit; did the grass outside his cage have a different flavour? Or perhaps, since we had not responded to him, he was saving face, was now showing us that of course he had not been reaching out to us at all, at all.

But as we turned away from the cage, he thrust his hands out towards us again; and followed us, padding after us as far as his commodious cage would let him, and then he pursued us further and further with his dreadful speaking eyes as we went off.

The nicer the zoo, the more terrible.

When darkness falls and the crowds are gone and the beasts inherit Regents Park, I should think the mandrills sometimes say to one another: 'Well, taking all things into consideration, how much better off we are here than in the wild! Nice food, regular meals, no predators, no snakes, free medical care, roofs over our heads ... and, after all this time, we couldn't really cope with the wild, again, could we?'

So they console themselves, perhaps. And, perhaps, weep.

*from* Nothing Sacred *by Angela Carter*

# CONFESSIONS OF A ZOO LOVER

Of course in the continents which still have a wide variety of wild fauna, use will be made of the natural settings; but for the future I believe that zoos will give us individual houses that reproduce ideal conditions for the creatures within them: houses that not only provide a spectacle for the visitor un-clouded by bars and wire, but also make possible for the animals the necessary withdrawal to solitude that will allow them to mate and breed in peace. Yet the parks in which the houses are placed will not, I believe, attempt to represent 'natural conditions'; they are far more likely to return to ornamental parks like those of the beautiful zoo at Lisbon, recalling the aristocratic origins of zoos as noblemen's pleasure gardens. This, of course, means a revival of zoos in the centres of cities, not only small collections like those in New York's Central Park, but the large elaborate zoos like those of Antwerp or Barcelona where only the occasional crash of brakes or the rattle of an electric train makes you realize that you are not, after all, far away in a limitless garden of Eden, but in the heart of a modern industrial town.

[. . .]

For city dwellers in Philadelphia, New York, or Berlin, or for small nations with an ever-shrinking countryside like England or Holland, the zoo is increasingly the only means left of learning some respect and humility before other than human ways of living; the only means of learning pleasure in the existence of what is not the same as ourselves, and so perhaps learning more tolerance of other human beings with different noses, colours or smells.

*from* Reflections in a Writer's Eye *by Angus Wilson*

## Suggestions for writing

1 Write an article that uses this material to give *both* views of the zoo debate. Your article must give a balanced account of the arguments. You will need:

(a) a good headline

(b) an interesting introduction

(c) quotes from the experts and the writers

(d) a conclusion that sums up the arguments but *does not* give your own views.

2 Create a publicity campaign either for or against zoos. As part of your campaign:

(a) design a handbill or pamphlet (use the photographs that accompany this unit to help you)

(b) write the transcript of a radio interview with yourself as spokesperson

**3** Use Angela Carter's idea of the zoo after dark, 'when the beasts inherit Regent's Park', as the basis for a story in which the animals discuss their imprisonment and debate whether they would be better off if they escaped and returned to the wild. You could make your writing humorous.

If you want more information, here are two useful addresses:

Zoocheck
Tempo House
15 Falcon Road
London SW11

The Royal Zoological Society
London Zoo
Regent's Park
London NW1

# *Animals – what rights should be accorded to them?*

The issues discussed in the following articles are obviously related to many of the ideas explored in the zoo debate above so you may wish to link these sections together. However, the question of our attitude to animals is much wider than whether we continue to run zoos or not. Brigid Brophy and Germaine Greer express views here which go right to the heart of the matter. Do we have the right to inflict pain on animals?

# *CAA*

Every year thousands of our fellow inhabitants of Britain are tricked, tortured, mutilated and killed. None of the main political parties opposes this. One major party explicitly supports the practice and promises that, should it win the next general election, it will subsidise the tortures from public funds. The fellow beings of ours at whom this conspiracy is aimed are fish.

Fish have a peculiar effect on humans. That is through no fault of the fish. The fish in our rivers, reservoirs and so forth constitute no danger to us. There is not a single recorded

instance where a human, walking by the side of a canal, has been subjected to unprovoked aggression by a fish leaping out of the water and attacking him or trying to drag him in and drown him.

It is we who are the unprovoked aggressors. Walk a mile along a canal bank in Britain and you will see dozens of humans lurking, one by one, in elaborate, expensive and stealthy ambush, dangling in front of the fish what purports to be a free meal but is really the most painful of entrapments, a hook through the lip.

None of these people would offer a child or a dog a bar of chocolate that in fact concealed a hook to be used, after a passage of drawn-out torture that is called, ironically, 'playing' him, to yank him to his death.

It is as though the fact that the fish are there in the water, for most of the time invisible to us, pursuing their own concerns, is something we insist on treating as an insult to us. Dozens of adult humans seem to feel challenged to prove that they are more cunning and more advanced in technology than a fish. Well, of course they are. No contest. Intellectually, it is the humans who are pathetic. But it is the fish who suffers and who is deprived of his life.

The peculiar effect that fish have on humans is to make them forget their humanity and much that goes with it: not only compassion but reason and knowledge.

Consider the sort of conversation I regularly have when a new acquaintance telephones with an invitation to dinner. In common courtesy, before I accept such an invitation I tell our prospective host or hostess that my husband and I are vegetarians. Close friends, of course, already know, and, as it happens, most of them, including our grown-up daughter, are vegetarians too. Indeed, now that vegetarianism is increasing so rapidly, it often turns out that the new host or hostess replies 'So are we' and no further dialogue is needed.

Otherwise, what then takes place goes like this.

'No problem', says host/hostess. 'We love cooking vegetables' or 'I'm particularly proud of my pasta'. That is often followed by 'As a matter of fact, I've often thought I'd like to be a vegetarian myself'.

This was a fashionable thing to say even before April of this year, when Paul McCartney extracted from the Duke of Edinburgh the news that it would not take much persuading to make Prince Charles a vegetarian. As a piece of conversation, however, I find it baffling. There is no shortage of vegetarian food in Britain. To be a vegetarian is the easiest thing in the world, as well as a pleasant one. It is certainly as healthy as being a carnivore and probably healthier, and, though I don't expect this will weigh with the Prince of Wales, it is much, much cheaper. If host/hostess wants to go vegetarian, what, I wonder, is stopping him/her?

Without explaining this point, host/hostess usually continues 'We'll see you on Friday, then. I look forward to cooking a vegetarian meal.' My hand moves to put down the receiver but is interrupted by 'Oh, by the way. You do eat fish, don't you?'

How, I wonder, have so many sane, knowledgeable, well-educated human beings managed to persuade themselves that a fish is a vegetable?

Or consider the Labour Party. I am a member of the Labour Party and I should naturally like to urge anyone I can to vote for it and, for preference, join it. In general I can urge this without violence to my conscience as a respecter of the rights of animals. For people who recognise that the love of liberty and fairness is claptrap unless you apply it to animals of every species and not just to animals of the human species in whom it is easy to see ourselves reflected, Labour policies stop short of the ideal. Even so, they are the best offered by a major party, and at least they identify the areas where reform is most urgently needed.

They promise priority to discovering and developing methods of scientific research that do not use (or, rather, abuse) animals, to stopping at least the most violent atrocities of 'intensive' farming (farming, that is, in concentration camps) and to introducing laws to ban all hunting with dogs.

In this last item you can hardly say that Labour has gone boldly out on an extremist limb. Opinion polls have been showing for the last ten years that 60 to 70 per cent of the population would welcome a law banning hunting. Still, the policy as a whole will provoke some flak, chiefly from those who make money from exploiting animals, and it is fair to say that Labour has bravely put reason and decency before electoral caution.

Turn, however, to another section of Labour's campaign document, 'The New Hope for Britain', and you run straight into the Fish Effect – the peculiar response of humans to fish. Labour, we are assured, 'will also provide for wider use of the countryside for recreational purposes, such as angling'. What has destruction to do with any form of creation, including recreation, and why do politicians suppose that people can't enjoy the countryside without causing death?

True, some anglers may be potential Labour voters. But then, so may some thugs who beat up old-age pensioners for fun. Is a political party not to say that beating up old-age pensioners is cruel for fear of losing the thug vote? Does any party want to be known as the self-contradictory party (spare foxes but condemn fish to death)? It is hypocritical to talk about the importance of education if you are scared to inform the citizens that fish are not vegetables or clockwork toys but sentient animals like you and me.

Fish are vertebrates like ourselves, though they extract oxygen from the water through gills whereas we extract it from the air through lungs. To be exposed to the air is distressing and ultimately fatal to them in the same way that having our heads forced under water is to us. They function, just as we do, through a brain and a nervous system. There is exactly as much reason to believe that fish feel distress and pain as there is to believe that dogs do or that our next-door neighbour does.

This point was made clearly by a panel that, after sitting for three years under the chairmanship of a zoologist, reported in 1980. The report condemned the cruelty of angling of both kinds.

One kind of angling impales the fish on a hook with the intention that he shall, after torture, die. (And he may not be the only animal to do so. Lines and weights are often left lying about that countryside that Labour wants us to enjoy, where they maim or poison mammals and birds.) The other kind, practised in 'coarse fishing' competitions, impales the fish, hooks him out of his habitat, and imprisons him, often in polluted water, until he has been handled, weighed and mea-sured to boost the angler's competitive ego, after which he is returned to the water he was taken from – very often to die of shock or, slowly, from injuries or infections caused by handling him.

Happily for the good name of the human species, a group was formed in the 1980s called the Campaign for the Abolition of Angling (whose address is PO Box 14, Romsey, SO5 9NN). As a new group, it is still small, but my hope is that enough people will join it (which costs very little) to exert an influence on all the parties, and that enough CAA members will then join the Labour Party to persuade it to change its ignorant and illogical mind about fish.

I once met an MP (of a different party) who believed he was a great friend to animals. He opposed all blood sports – except angling. He seriously assured me that fish have no feelings 'because they are cold-blooded'.

I do not think we can afford (and I know the fish cannot afford) legislators whose grasp on elementary biology is so sketchy that they suppose sensation to be transmitted by the temperature of the blood rather than by the nerve endings – with which, the

Cranbrook Report establishes, the lips and mouths of fish are 'well endowed'.

In scientific fact, it is a sensitive animal whose lip anglers pierce and whom they terrorise and do to death under the pretence of pursuing an innocent and laudable pastime, taking part in sport and enjoying the countryside.

The name 'coarse' is given to fish whose corpses do not make delicate eating for humans. But which is truly coarse: the fish or the bully who considers 'coarse fishing' a sport? And which is, in the most telling sense, 'cold-blooded': the fish or the human who tortures him?

*from* Baroque N' Roll *by Brigid Brophy*

## Group discussion

- With your group, make a list of the arguments against fishing that Brigid Brophy puts forward in this article. You could group them under headings such as 'Our attitude to fish' or 'Do fish feel pain?'.

- Explain the effectiveness of the opening of this article. Why does Brophy not mention the word fish in the title or until the end of the first paragraph?

- Discuss the use of humour in this article. Do you find parts of it funny and if so, does this make it more or less persuasive?

- In your group, discuss your attitudes to angling. It is the most popular participatory sport in the country, so it is quite likely that at least one of your group and a number of your class will have fished at some time. Do you find Brigid Brophy's arguments persuasive?

- Before reading Germaine Greer's article, take a large sheet of paper and write the word 'RAT' in the middle. In your group, discuss everything you associate with the word. Fill the sheet of paper with your ideas.

- Compare your findings with other groups – did you all come up with similar ideas?

  Now read the next article by Germaine Greer. It was written in the hot, dry summer of 1989 during which many parts of the country suffered from a dramatic increase in the rat population.

# RATS ARE ANIMALS, TOO

It must be at least a week since I've seen a rat, which could mean that the plague is over. Perhaps the Pied Piper went past one morning before we were up. The Pied Piper's method of musical entrapment is the only humane one that has ever been suggested for rats. For months now we have been involved in orgies of trapping, drowning, poisoning and even shooting of highly developed intelligent animals who have lived as close to man for the last few thousand years as dogs have. Rats are hard to kill; they resist; they fight and bite and scream, but no animal liberationist ever hears them.

No one has come snooping round our farms to see that we dispose of our rats in a humane fashion. We were far more likely to find ourselves in trouble for failing completely to exterminate the rats, for doing it inefficiently rather than for doing it in too brutal a fashion. There is probably something in the bye-laws that says we could be prosecuted for failing to paralyse, blind, and corrode the guts out of our rats. Certainly we could not have sold eggs or chickens when there were rat droppings all over the hen-house and rat holes all around the walls, and rats sitting up in broad daylight eating the hens' pellets as well as rats stealing the eggs. The upshot of inspection would probably have been slaughter of the hens as well as the rats.

The cats caught the younger rats, and killed them with a bite on the back of the neck. They left them meticulously uneaten, not even nibbled, on the front doormat, so that we could see how pretty a young, unmarked rat can be, with delicate pink hands and feet and a glossy mud-brown coat. We humans were less efficient. We left poisoned baits of various kinds, and then agonised over how long the rats would take to die, especially after they ate their way through the poisoned corn bin and 20 lbs of poisoned corn in one night. Then we realised that the rats had grown resistant to that poison and the 10 other brands that we subsequently tried. Someone suggested gassing them, and for all I know someone may have tried, but as the rat network ran for miles through the rubble that runs the length of my land, we couldn't be sure the gas wouldn't come out in a dangerous place, come sneaking into the cellar and up the stairs, or bubbling through the cisterns.

Traps were the worst, for the rats dragged them all over the place, panting and wailing. They couldn't be got out of them because they fought and bit, so we gave up and threw the traps, rat and all, into the water butt. I had heard that the humane way to put an end to the misery of trapped rats was to drop them into boiling water, so that they die instantaneously from shock, but no one had the stomach for that. So they struggled around the water butt with a trap around their necks for an hour or two, and we all kept well away until the next day, when the traps were fished out and baited again.

If animals have rights, then rats have rights, but there is no rat ombudsman. If it is a gross infringement of an animal's rights to kill it, why do we have a duty to kill rats? Because they spread disease? So do most of the other animals that live in close proximity to man; rats don't spread more disease than pigs, and perhaps no more than that most hallowed of all animal parasites, the dog. They certainly make reparation for the disease they spread by the sterling service they offer in our laboratories, which represents the only case in which rats must be humanely killed.

For people who live in towns, killing is an exotic concept; they are the people who feel that the object that the foetus is 'alive' is an argument against killing it, when in fact it is the necessary condition for killing it. People who live in the country have to observe killing at every turn. The first time I saw 50 rooks clean out my beech trees, chattering lazily in the uppermost branches as they snacked off fledglings grown to a toothsome size, I felt quite sick with horror. Now I am used to it. The first time a racing pigeon came down in my hen run for a drink and a beakful of corn, only to be torn apart by my hens until there was only a pair of silver wings left to show what had become of him, I felt that I hated my hens. But when I heard the rabbit screaming a few weeks ago, when the stoat had it cornered, I watched to see the kill, which was elegant in its utter merciless-ness. Yesterday I found the stoat, a parchment stoat under a drift of pinkish fluff. He had been killed but not eaten by a competing carnivore. A mink, perhaps, the descendant of some liberated before I came to this place. (Liberating minks is damn stupid, especially if you are concerned for the endangered species, for minks kill without discrimination or appetite.)

Animal rights must include the right to kill, and to kill messily, for sport or just to get the gastric juices flowing, or to clear the ground for an imperialist takeover by a single species. Man is an animal, you might argue, and therefore has the right to kill other animals in all the ways that they kill each other. This it seems is not right; man is to be superior to the other animals and stop killing them for sport or fur or any other reason. He is evidently not to breed them or farm them either.

The logic of animal rights seems at least questionable. The propaganda deals only with appealing creatures, whales, tigers, lynxes, seal pups and natterjack toads. When the RSPCA tried to alert people to the suffering caused by overbreeding of dogs, by showing a huge heap of dogs, all killed humanely, the picture was considered too harrowing to be seen. Millions of rats were ineptly tortured to death in the same period, but the common perception is that they got no more than they deserved. To rats at least animal liberation must seem pure humbug.

*from the* Independent *magazine, 5 August 1989*

## Group discussion

- Make a list of words and phrases used in the article to describe rats. Put it next to your original 'RAT' sheet – how do they compare?
- In your group, discuss your attitudes to animal rights. You will need to consider the following:

  factory farming
  vegetarianism
  vivisection
  hunting

Here are some statements to help you focus your discussion. Which of these do you agree with?

(a) Killing animals is wrong under any circumstances.
(b) Eating meat is natural for human beings.
(c) Using animals for medical research is acceptable.
(d) A vegetarian diet is perfectly healthy.
(e) Killing animals for sport gets rid of people's natural aggression.
(f) If we want cheap food we must accept factory farming.

Work towards writing a statement which expresses the position of your group on the issue. If there is serious disagreement then you may need to write more than one statement.

## *Suggestions for writing*

1 Put forward your own views on the subject of animal rights in the form of an article for a newspaper or magazine aimed at your age-group or slightly younger. Use quotes from the articles you have read to back up your arguments. Remember to think of a powerful headline and be as persuasive as you can.

If you want more information, here are two useful addresses:

Animal Liberation Front
PO Box 190
8 Elm Avenue
Nottingham

Compassion in World Farming
Lyndum House
High Street
Petersfield
Hampshire

2 Produce a leaflet to promote the CAA. Use extracts from Bridget Brophy's article alongside your own writing and graphics to produce a persuasive leaflet. You will need to search out some effective photographs.

OR

Perhaps you are a keen angler. If so, produce a leaflet that promotes the benefits of angling. Focus on the ways in which fishing benefits the environment and its value as peaceful recreation. If you need more information you could write to:

The British Field Sports Society
59 Kennington Road
Guildford
Surrey
GUI 3SF

# Television – is it bad for children?

Every child loves television and, it seems, every adult thinks that television is bad for children. We have all grown up being told to 'switch off the box and go out and get some fresh air', or warned that we will get 'square eyes' from watching 'the goggle box'. The question remains, though, 'Is television bad for children?'

One of the main criticisms of children's television viewing is that it prevents them from reading. The following passages discuss this allegation, Christina Hardyment argues in an article for the *Independent* that, because of television, children are 'screened off from the joys of literature'.

# SCREENED OFF FROM THE JOYS OF LITERATURE

### *CHRISTINA HARDYMENT ON TELEVISION'S THREAT TO THE ART OF READING*

In Ray Bradbury's fantasy of the future, *Fahrenheit 451*, a passive population watches wall-to-wall television while firemen burn books – all literature is subversive and banned by the government. His version should touch a tender nerve in parents. Two-thirds of British children's week-day leisure time is spent watching television – roughly three hours a day. This weekly average of 23 hours is twice as much time as their parents spent in front of the box as children 30 years ago, albeit a trifle less than the 29 hours the average adult now watches each week.

There is surprisingly little up-to-date British research on television's effect on reading, and there is more opinion than fact in the statements made by both advocates and critics of television. What is ascertainable, and will be good news for parents, is that watching television does not appear to have much effect on the initial acquisition of reading skills. But what happens next? How do readers become booklovers?

Enthusiasts for television such as psychologist Maire Messenger Davies point to the high quality of British TV and argue that television actually encourages reading. Sales of books featured on TV will double or triple for the duration of the series, and many such books are just what traditionalists like to see their children reading – *Chronicles of Narnia*, *My Family and Other Animals* or *Tom's Midnight Garden*. Davies believes that television complements reading rather than displacing it. 'One avid 15-year-old reader explained: "When I've enjoyed something like *Gone with the Wind* on television, or as a film, I can't wait to read the book, just to find our more about the characters."'

TV can certainly lead children to heavyweight classics that they would not have approached on their own. On the other hand, it can also create disappointments. Children habituated to visual spoonfeeding may find their low opinion of books being confirmed by the oldfashioned language of, say, *Anne of Green Gables*. And, for all Davies's *Gone With the Wind* anecdote, in my experience it is more common for children to refuse to read a book that they've seen televised.

Roald Dahl, the best-selling children's author of the decade, is not happy about TV, as his memorable three-page rhyming diatribe on the subject in *Charlie and the Chocolate Factory* made clear ('It rots the senses in the head! / It kills imagination dead! / It clogs and clutters up the mind! / It makes a child so dull and blind. / His powers of thinking rust and freeze! / He cannot think – he only sees!'). Dahl takes the robust old-fashioned view that parents should limit the amount of time their children watch television, and encourage them to play games, make things, and above all to read. 'My passion in life is to teach children to acquire the habit of reading a book – not just a comic or newspaper. To ensure that books are no longer daunting to them parents should choose exciting ones and start reading them to their children. If you can give children a book that is so exciting and so funny that they really enjoy it and feel at home with it, that will serve them enormously well in life.'

Susan Prest, who teaches North Oxford juniors, is also pessimistic about the effect of television of children's literacy. 'In the last 20 years I've witnessed a very marked downward spiral in the length of time children spend reading, and also in the length of the books they choose to read. The nine-year-olds are less and less literate, they're also much less adventurous readers, and I'm sure that's because it's infinitely easier to flop in front of the television than to get into a worthwhile book'.

Booksellers have mixed feelings about television. 'Children are certainly reading less. But a new children's TV series always brings parents we haven't seen before into the bookshop. Once they're in the shop, they may well pick up something else,' said David Taylor, marketing manager of the Blackwell Retail Group. Taylor values his young customers very highly indeed. 'After all, they are our adult customers of the future.'

At the moment, children's bookshops and libraries are over-flowing with attractively presented, high-quality literature for children – not just the old classics that parents remember fondly, but sparky, creative writing that could inspire children with a deep respect for the written word. But this happy situation may not last. Performers in our enterprise economy have to get results from their investments. More and more bookshops are being driven to exploit character merchandising techniques previously associated with toys. A new Dr Who 'novel' is published every month. 'The TV tie-in edition is a powerful selling tool' commented Sue Berger of Puffin. 'It brings the book to people's attention because booksellers are more willing to display it.'

Does it really matter that children are getting their culture through a screen instead of the written word? I think it does. In the long run, after all, reading means independence of thought. There aren't many educational tasks left to parents these days, but instilling that 'habit of reading' which Dahl believes in is among the most important. We have to be prepared to promote interest in books far beyond the flurry of interest that surrounds the five-year-old's first nervous spelling out of syllables. We need to pull out the plug of the TV, take children to bookshops and libraries, encourage them to be critical about what they find there, and lobby to keep up the standards that exist.

It is certainly far easier to leave them (and ourselves) in front of the TV, especially when coming home late after a day at work. But consider what we are set to lose. It is no use relying on the present high quality of British television. Although the Government has qualified the free-for-all of its initial White Paper on Broadcasting, there are still no guarantees that we are not approaching a *Fahrenheit 451* age when wall-to-wall brightspeak for the masses will replace the priceless individuality of literature.

*from the* Independent, *8 July 1989*

Now read this extract from Dr Maire Messenger Davies's book *Television is Good For Your Kids.* From the title of the book it is not very difficult to guess what line Dr Davies is going to take.

# TV SPIN-OFFS

## TELEVISION AND BOOKS

A common concern about the side-effects of television is that it stops children reading. A study carried out by Susan Neuman in the United States in 1984 took measurements of time spent watching television in over two million children – aged nine, 13 and 17 – in eight different states, and compared these measurements of viewing hours with measurements of reading skills in school, and with children's use and enjoyment of reading as a leisure activity. These comparisons were subjected to a number of computer analyses, taking into account sex, ethnic background and socio-economic status, and no overall relationship was found between reading skills, leisure reading and television watching. In other words, for the sample as a whole, the amount of television watching did not relate to being a good or a bad reader (as measured by comprehension, vocabulary and study skills in school) nor did it relate to how much children did, or did not, read in their leisure time. If television stopped children from reading for pleasure, or from learning to read, we would expect that, the more television they watched, the poorer would be their reading performance, and the less they would read for pleasure. This study found no such relationships.

There were some interesting variations within the sample. For instance, the results revealed that children who watched a moderate amount of TV (between two and three hours a day) had higher reading achievement scores than children who watched less (although this was less likely to be so in California and Rhode Island, for some unknown reason). When it came to time spent reading for pleasure, again no relationship was found between longer hours spent watching television and fewer hours spent reading. In one group – nine-year-olds – there was actually a positive relationship: that is, the more they watched television, the more they read.

A more recent study, involving 13,000 11- to 16-year-olds in Britain in which researchers at Exeter University focused on one evening's activities, found a similar unexpected relationship between heavy viewing (five or more hours) and increased amounts of reading (two or more hours spent reading for pleasure). Among less heavy viewers and readers there was no relationship at all to suggest that the more children watched, the less they read. With both boys and girls, book reading declined in the older age groups (perhaps reflecting an increasing amount of homework), and television viewing also declined among girls, but not among boys. The authors stress that the relationship between different leisure-time activities is a complex one which varies for different reasons. Their study only asked about the previous evening. Viewing habits obviously vary over time and it may be that other patterns would be forthcoming on different nights of the week, or at other times of the year. Nevertheless, such a large sample provides fairly convincing evidence of the lack of support for the 'displacement' theory of television's effects on reading.

Susan Neuman argues that children are motivated to read, or to watch television, not because of the time available (or not available) but because of enjoyment: 'When students defined reading as an enjoyable activity, they tended to do more reading during their free time.' Neuman points out that:

> Children enjoy television and often do not enjoy reading. Instead of blaming television for this phenomenon, it makes sense to try and change this attitude ... We must develop ways to extend their understanding of its [reading's] compelling uses outside the school setting.

## BOOKS AND THE BOX

A variety of ways of persuading children of the 'compelling uses' of reading was explored at a conference called 'Books and the Box' held in London in February 1988 by the Children's Book Circle, at which TV producers, writers, performers, market researchers and representatives of the book and toy trade, met to consider 'the relationship between children, books and television.' Children's author Helen Cresswell, who has written a number of series for television, including *Polly Flint* (ITV Central) and *Moondial* (BBC), argued that writing for television had made her a better writer:

*Polly Flint* was the first decent novel I ever wrote. I didn't know the meaning of the word 'plot' until I wrote *Polly Flint*. Writing a serial for television meant that there had to be at least five points in the story when something had to happen to make people turn on next week.

Helen Cresswell described this process as 'television doing the book world a favour'. She pointed out that the process of writing both the TV scripts and the book of *Polly Flint* side by side was 'a new art form'. She has 'always been delighted with the TV versions of my books. Something is added rather than subtracted. Actors can give characters a depth and strength not in the book. The production of *Moondial* gave it a depth and strength not in the book.'

Both *Moondial* and *Polly Flint* have been successful paperbacks. Televising a dramatised version of an existing book can hugely increase its sales in the shops. When Eric Hill's *Spot* books were televised, their publisher, Heinemann, found that sales of the books doubled from 10,000 to 20,000 in a year. The sales of *Thomas the Tank Engine* books doubled from 20,000 to 40,000 when the series was shown on ITV.

Paul Stone, a drama producer for the BBC, who also spoke at the conference, pointed out that the television/publishing relationship can work both ways. He had commissioned distinguished children's writers such as Leon Garfield and Bernard Ashley to write original drama serials especially for children's BBC – *December Rose* and *Running Scared* respectively. They were very different kinds of story. *December Rose* was a historical adventure about a cockney chimney sweep who became involved in political corruption, set against a background of life on a river barge. *Running Scared* was a contemporary story, set in the East End of London, about an English girl and her Asian friend becoming involved in a protection racket, with the theme of racial prejudice and misunderstanding running through it. Book versions of both became best-sellers.

Having a book dramatised on television is a guaranteed way to increase its sales. It will also dramatically increase the number of borrowings from libraries. Angela Beeching, executive producer of the BBC's *Jackanory* (the storytelling programme) has been asked by librarians throughout the country to give them advance warning of what books will be featured in the series, so that they can make sure these books are in stock. Evidence like this suggests that television, far from preventing children from reading, can act as a powerful stimulus to reading. Television has also revived the art and power of direct storytelling – *Jackanory* being a long-running example. At the conference, actor and storyteller Tony Robinson described how he had developed his own technique of semi-improvised television storytelling, as in his dramatic rendering of *The Odyssey* for children's television. He had seen the excitement of direct narrative when rehearsing for a National Theatre production of *The Oresteia* and the actors had had to tell some of the text in their own words; and behind masks: 'The masks appeared to change at key dramatic moments in the text.' For Robinson, story telling is about 'excitement and passion', of which the immediacy of direct improvisation to the camera, rather than reading from an autocue, is a part. Again, the book version sold well. One child I know, who was only eight years old, loved it so much that he asked the librarian for a copy of Homer's original.

The key to explaining this ability of television to stimulate children into reading book versions of TV stories may well be the enjoyment factor, mentioned by Susan Neuman. Watching a series on television clearly does not put children off wanting to go through the story again. On the contrary, they repeat the enjoyable experience by reading the book. This desire to follow up a story, of which they already know the outcome, in book form, further suggests that children are well able to perceive the distinctions between the pleasures of television viewing and those of reading: they are different kinds of enjoyment and one is not a substitute for the other. One avid 15-year-old reader explained: 'When I've enjoyed something on television, or as a film, I can't wait to read the book, just to find out more about all the characters.' She cited *Gone with the Wind* as an example: 'I enjoyed the book more than the film, because there was so much more detail and depth in it.' Thus, the pleasures of reading and viewing are not mutually exclusive. Rather, they appear to be complementary to each other. If this is generally so, it helps to explain the findings (mentioned above) that children who watch a lot of television also read a lot. The evidence described here suggests that television does not displace reading. It provides a different form of satisfaction which can both complement and help to promote reading.

There are still, as there always have been, large numbers of children who do not, and will not, read for pleasure no matter how great the encouragement of parents and teachers. One such group has traditionally been boys of all ages, but particularly adolescent boys. In 1987, the Book Trust mounted a television campaign aimed at older teenagers called 'Let's throw the book at you', in which advertisements on London Weekend Television, using popular youth presenter Jonathan Ross as front-man, promoted the idea of reading as 'a generic activity'. No particular book, or publisher, was featured but viewers were invited to phone in for a free book and a 'Top 40' list of books. Four and a half thousand phone calls were received in response to the first promotion on 30th October, and a further three thousand came in after repeats of the 'commercial' in the next two days. Ten per cent of the first group of calls (460) came from under-16s, and of these, the majority were boys. Sixty five per cent of those wanting humorous books were boys; 60 per cent of requests for music books were from boys and 80 per cent of requests for science fiction came from boys. Lindsay Pearson, projects manager of the Book Trust, who spoke at the Books and the Box conference, was surprised at this breakdown, in view of boys' traditional resistance to reading as a pastime. She felt that this form of televised promotion was an excellent way of getting boys to show an interest in books.

*from* Television is Good for Your Kids *by*
*Maire Messenger Davies*

# Group discussion

- Christina Hardyment says that 'There is surprisingly little up-to-date British research on television's effect on reading'. Dr Davies's research seems to show that TV sells books. In your group discuss the ways in which your viewing and reading are related. Here are some questions to help you to focus your discussion.

  (a) Have you ever read a book because you enjoyed the television version?

  (b) Would you have read the book anyway?

  (c) How many hours do you spend reading per week?

  (d) How many hours do you spend watching TV?

  (e) Do you read more or less than you used to?

  (f) Do you buy books?

You could extend this discussion by devising a questionnaire to be filled in by other pupils to find out if there is a relationship between the amount of TV watching and reading they do. It would be most interesting if you questioned a sample of first, third and fifth year students to see how their habits change.

- A number of famous and popular books are mentioned in these articles. Have you heard of them all or read some of them? Discuss the books you remember from your early reading years (including books read to you). Do you share any books with other members of your group? There may even be one or two books that everyone remembers.

  Share your findings with the rest of the class. Are there any firm favourites?

- Christina Hardyment's article is full of statements that denigrate television and elevate reading. She obviously believes that TV is harmful and reading is 'improving'. Go through her article and pick out the phrases that imply this view – for instance 'the priceless individuality of literature'.

  Discuss whether you feel that books are superior to television. Remember, all new inventions are regarded suspiciously at first. Will your grandchildren ever read a book and, if not, does it matter?

- Later in her book, Dr Davies writes about the fond way in which we look back on the television programmes that we watched as children. Just as we all have reading histories, we also have TV watching histories. Which programmes do you remember from your childhood? Discuss them in your group. Are there any that everyone seems to have enjoyed?

  Share the results of your discussion with the rest of the class.

## Suggestions for writing

1 If you have carried out the survey suggested above then write up your findings. Are any of the results surprising or do they confirm the results of surveys quoted in Dr Davies's article?

  Use the articles and the results of your survey to write your own article on the relationship between TV and reading, paying particular reference to your own age group.

2 Write your 'reading autobiography'. That is a history of your experience of reading from the first stories you can remember hearing to the books you read now. Explain how your tastes have changed and what made you read the books you have enjoyed. Do

you have a pet hate (some people cannot stand science fiction, for example) or a great obsession?

3 Write your 'TV watching autobiography' in which you describe the programmes that most influenced your childhood. Did you use the characters in your games and act out the stories with your friends? Are there signature tunes or particular phrases that bring back memories for you? End your writing with a description of the kind of television you enjoy watching now.

# Acknowledgements

The publishers would like to thank the following for permission to reproduce material in this volume:

Aitken and Stone Ltd for 'Rats Are Animals, Too' by Germaine Greer; Sally Brampton for her article 'The Golden Time'; Jonathan Cape Ltd for 'I Was a Playboy Bunny' from *Outrageous Acts and Everyday Rebellions* by Gloria Steinem; Centerprise Trust Ltd for the extract from *Jackie's Story*; Chatto and Windus for 'On the Edge of a Foreign City' from *The White Bird* by John Berger; Collins Publishers for the extract from *Dressing for Breakfast* by Stephanie Calman; Buchi Emecheta for 'Pussy Cat Mansions' from *In the Ditch*; English Tourist Board for the extract from *Bradford Mini Guide*; Faber and Faber Ltd for the extracts from *My Left Foot* by Shane Connaughton and Jim Sheridan; Granta Publications Ltd for the extract from *White Into Black* by Martha Gellhorn and *Bradford* by Hanif Kureishi; Paul Hamann for his article 'Last Days on Death Row'; Hamish Hamilton Ltd for 'CAA' from *Baroque 'N' Roll* by Bridget Brophy, © Bridget Brophy 1985; William Heinemann Ltd for the extract from *The Blindfold Horse* by Shusha Guppy, © 1988 by Shusha Guppy; Institute for the Study of Drug Dependence for 'It Seems Like The Sky Falls In' from *Coping With a Nightmare*; Michael Joseph Ltd for the extract from *Inside Out* by Rosie Johnston, © Rosie Johnston 1989; Newspaper Publishing Plc for 'Screened off From the Joys of Literature' by Christina Hardyment, *The Independent*, 8 July, 1989; Peters Fraser and Dunlop Group Ltd for 'Girls' Careers' from *The Way We Live Now* by Polly Toynbee; Schocken Books, Inc. for the extract from 'The Shop' from *Burning Lights* by Bella Chagall, © 1946 by Schocken Books Inc., published by Pantheon Books, a division of Random House, Inc.; Martin Secker and Warburg for 'The Letter "A"' and 'A Look of Pity' from *My Left Foot* by Christy Brown, © 1954 by Christy Brown; Serpent's Tail for 'Turan' from *Under a Crescent Moon* by Daniel de Souza and the extracts from *Diary 1964–85* by Ian Breakwell; Hilary Shipman Ltd for 'It Is Good for Your Children' from *Television Is Good For Your Kids* by Marie Messenger-Davies (1989); Unwin Hyman Ltd/Melanie Jackson Agency for the extract from *What Do You Care What Other People Think* by Richard Feynman, © 1988 Gwyneth Feynman and Ralph Leighton; George Weidenfeld and Nicolson Ltd for 'I've Cracked It' from *Under the Eye of the Clock* by Christopher Nolan; George Weidenfeld and Nicolson/Jazz Workshop Inc. for the extract from *Beneath the Underdog* by Charles Mingus.

Every effort has been made to trace and acknowledge ownership of copyright. The publishers will be glad to make suitable arrangements with any copyright holders whom it has not been possible to contact.